The Sands of Erebus

Drew Gardner

PublishAmerica
Baltimore

© 2006 by Drew Gardner.
All rights reserved. No part of this book may be reproduced, stored in a retrieval system or transmitted in any form or by any means without the prior written permission of the publishers, except by a reviewer who may quote brief passages in a review to be printed in a newspaper, magazine or journal.

First printing

At the specific preference of the author, PublishAmerica allowed this work to remain exactly as the author intended, verbatim, without editorial input.

All characters appearing in this work are fictitious. Any resemblance to real persons, living or dead, is purely coincidental.

ISBN: 1-4241-3908-2
PUBLISHED BY PUBLISHAMERICA, LLLP
www.publishamerica.com
Baltimore

Printed in the United States of America

Acknowledgements

Books:

Stevens, John. *The Secrets of Aikido*. Boston: Shambhala Publications, Inc. 1995.

Song Lyrics:

Cretu, Michael. "Samurai." *The Invisible Man.* Virgin 1985.

Enigma. "The Child In Us." *Le Roi Est Mort, VIVE Le Roi!* Virgin 1996.

Enigma. "Why!" *Le Roi Est Mort, VIVE Le Roi!* Virgin 1996.

South Beach

"A beach is an edge, a limit defining the ground whereupon a man can walk no farther. Yet there is no distinct line of boundary—for a while a man can both walk and swim as the water deepens gradually."
∧ *from* the short story *Solid Meets Liquid* by Jackson Muldoone

Go for the Gold was printed within Olympic rings on a sandy black towel. Next to it lay a gray tee shirt with *Florida State Seminoles* printed in garnet across the front. Twenty steps away from these objects stood Jackson, near the waves of Miami's South Beach. His feet were upon those smoothest of sands—the kind periodically splashed by incoming waves of saltwater. He gathered a mild sense of clarity while breathing deeply of the wholesome, pungent air.

The last reaches of a wave washed over his feet and loosened the temporary foundation beneath him. As it receded, the wave pulled him slightly closer to the Atlantic Ocean. While he stabilized his stance, he remembered something one of his high school English teachers once shared with the class.

"If you ever want to feel truly insignificant, face the ocean. The sheer vastness can humble anyone."

Every schoolteacher I've had has offered profound insights, he thought, *enriching his or her students beyond the scope of standard subject material. I'm six feet taller than these waters, all the way to the horizon and beyond. Ah, but could I swim to Morocco and back without being late for dinner? When I was a kid I'd run through the sand at full sprint into the ocean. Once my legs were in the water, I couldn't go more than five strides before collapsing face-first with a splash.* Without a second thought, he ran into the water and fell forward on his fifth stride. *Mmm...saltwater...tasty...trillions of gallons of it surround me...humbling indeed.*

It was the year 2001. Jackson Brandon Muldoone, known most commonly as "Jack", was a senior at the Florida State University in the city of Tallahassee. During a break from school, he was staying in Miami with his family. His three years at college had been a challenging and enjoyable rite of passage.

Jack was an only child. His mother's parents were born in Germany, and his father's parents were born in Ireland. Jack and his parents were all born in Miami. Throughout grade school, Jack went to church each Sunday with his family. They attended a Methodist church composed mostly of amiable, faithful worshippers.

Since early childhood, Jack befriended so many people of other cultural and religious backgrounds that it was hard for him to believe in the sovereign righteousness of the Protestant Church. The more Catholic, Hindu, Jewish, Muslim, Taoist, Buddhist, Shinto, agnostic, and atheist people he befriended, the less *correct* his church seemed. In Miami, white Anglo-Saxon Protestants comprised a minority of the city's population. Affected by the melting pot in which he lived, he stopped attending church and instead kept his mind in search of a religion of all religions. One practice he found highly spiritual was going to the beach by himself. He went alone because he wanted no distractions.

After swimming back to the shoreline, then facing the endless Atlantic, one word in particular kept surfacing from his subconscious—*senior. I'll be out in the working world in only a year*, he realized. *Do I face tears and toil from graduation till retirement?*

What can I do to ensure happiness on the road ahead? When will I find the woman of my dreams? The future is almost completely out of my control. I'm hardly more in charge of my destiny than a Portuguese man-o-war floating mindlessly far out there on the ocean surface.

Fear and helplessness did not always plague Jack's mind, though. Often during his moments of solitude facing the blinding ocean surface at sunrise, he could see hope through squinted eyelids. He experienced a consistent memory flow of great times spent with friends, family, and those former girlfriends toward whom he felt no bitterness. Bad memories strove to bury themselves in his subconscious, often in vain.

Ocean retreats had actually been quite rare for Jack; they were certainly not as common as simple meditations or drives in his car—a dark blue Ford Probe. The car's stereo system often played at reasonably high volumes, sending sound waves thorough Jackson's ears and igniting emotions in his brain. Much of his enjoyment in trips to the beach lay in the twenty-minute journey there and back.

Without warning, a soft, unidentified flying object struck Jack's arm. He looked down to see a small, colorful ball made of heavy foam.

"Sorry, sir," said a small girl nearby.

"Sir," he thought. "Didn't hurt a bit," he said. Then he laughed to himself. He tossed the ball back to the girl and noticed that she was playing catch with another young girl. One was black and the other white, but each other's skin color seemed to be the furthest thing from their minds. A brief moment of hope came over him as he thought, *There's Dr. Martin Luther King, Jr.'s Great Dream coming to fruition. Little black girls holding hands with little white girls. Dr. King deserves to be standing where I am...he would feel a sense of accomplishment and fulfillment.*

Jack was a twenty-two year old white man who didn't like to paint or be painted with a skin-color brush. He had known kind, generous people of an infinite palette of skin tones, so racial prejudgment was a shortcut he fought to avoid. It sometimes took every ounce of his willpower to keep the unhealthy aspects of association psychology in check, for he believed that each person deserved the benefit of the doubt. He wanted to receive the benefit of the doubt in return. He knew he could never work from a blank page with everyone, for some let automatic associations control their lives. He likened those people to electricity, following the uncivilized path of least mental resistance. He wished he could explain to racists that the melanin pigment skin gradient never begins with white nor ends with black. *Everyone's color is somewhere in-between,* he thought, *and our own skin tone identically matches that of no other.* Jack was a thinker, and thoughtless people of rash judgment frustrated him immensely.

Jack looked at the untainted joy of the two girls playing catch, and then he shifted his gaze toward the horizon with a Mona Lisa-like smile. He noticed a red and black cargo freighter in the distance. A momentary curiosity overtook him: *What's on board that moving warehouse? There could be ten thousand types of cargo or more in the manifest. That ship might've been at sea for months...how does the crew keep high spirits with such a lifestyle?*

Before Jack's contemplation of the ship could stay him too long, he realized that the timer on the parking meter was probably approaching zero. He turned around and headed for his towel. Feeling the sand beneath his feet brought to his mind a vision of himself walking in a giant hourglass, each step forcing the sand faster down into the chamber below. *Everyone begins with ten thousand grains of sand,* he thought. He noticed a small pile of sand burying the words "Go for the Gold" on his towel, and he paused for a moment to think. *Chasing riches can get us caught in the bottom chamber—if we place monetary wealth before love, we become blinded by the falling sands and we are left unable to perceive miracles.* He grinned half-heartedly, slung the towel over his shoulder, and grabbed the tee shirt in his right hand. He chuckled at the word silk-screened on his shirt.

Seminoles, he thought. *I'm not of Seminole or any other Native American descent, so am I attending the wrong university? Then again, I know an English girl among the "Fighting Irish". On that note, I'd be surprised to discover "stormy petrel" seeking four-year degrees at Oglethorpe University.*

Jack crossed a boardwalk, then the famed Ocean Drive, and he continued heading toward Bessy. She was a proud lady—a streamlined, aerodynamic, dark blue Ford Probe with a thick, silver racing-stripe painted over her centerline. She could accelerate rapidly and had a top-speed begging for a ride on the Autobahn. After about a half-mile walk from the beach, Jack rendezvoused with his car. *There's one of the most important ladies in my life*, he thought. *Bessy, ha-ha, named after Robby's car.*

Jack lived in a dormitory throughout his first year of college. His floor supervisor, known as a resident assistant, was a junior at F.S.U. and had befriended Jack soon after his arrival. They often played basketball and had some intellectual conversations. Most of their talks were about girls, while a few delved into global issues and the meaning of life.

During a thunderstorm one night, Jack drove his resident assistant, Robby, to his car at a distant parking lot. Upon arrival, Robby said, "There's Bessy Sue." After short-lived laughter, Jack realized he should likewise name his car "Bessy" out of respect and for remembrance of his friend. Jack often did peculiar things on a whim. He rarely called the car by her name aloud, but if anyone asked him whether or not he had a name for his car, he would reply, "Bessy," then pat the dashboard a few times. There were many subtle ways in which he could keep a small reminder of past friends. He found it essential to time and again remember good people whom he once knew, people who were blazing their separate trails.

Jack pressed the unlock button on his key chain, wondering only for an instant: *How does Bessy, even when out of sight, respond to this remote button? Technology amazes me to no end. I love Bessy, but I'm gonna have to find a girl with just two wheels soon. And I don't mean a motorcycle.* He climbed into the driver seat and headed home. Gliding down the interstate, Jack shifted gears and pondered the factory-bestowed name of his car. *Probe*, he thought, *that name fits my car's purpose to perfection. This vehicle carries me to destinations where I can consider—analyze—explore. En route to these places, music submerses my fears and self-doubt into the oceanic trenches of my subconscious.*

Humble Abode

"The spoils of an extravagant mansion become counter-valuable if they usurp the throne of comfort."
^ *from* the short story *When a House is a Home* by
Jackson Muldoone

    A medium-sized house with a swimming pool and palm tree landscaping patiently awaited Jack's return. He pulled onto the driveway and went inside. He greeted his mother then walked into his room. He sat in his cushioned desk chair, leaned back, and turned on the TV. Failing to find anything on besides commercials and soap operas, he peered around his room in boredom. Catching his eye first were a wooden sword and staff leaning against the wall. These were weapons he used in practicing Aikido, a Japanese martial art. In search of both a hobby and a new general direction in life, Jack had discovered an Aikido organization at his university during his sophomore year. More than a mere leisure activity, Aikido had become immensely influential in molding and refining his character.
    As a product of Jack's martial arts enthusiasm came a strong interest in Eastern religion and tradition. He turned and noticed scattered signs of Eastern influence in various parts of his room. On one shelf stood a

book on Buddhism entitled *The Compass of Zen*. On the walls hung a yin-and-yang poster, a certificate of advancement in Aikido, and a calligraphy painting of the Japanese character "hikari", which translates as "light".

This brushed character meant a great deal to Jackson. Literally translated, Aikido means "the way of harmony with energy." While this is the overview of Aikido, Jack felt the purpose and outcome of the training was to harness hikari. He could sometimes use this light to chase away his fears and insecurities, like a newly lit lantern might send a cockroach scurrying at full speed into obscurity. He leaned back in his desk chair and thought, *One day, perhaps, I'll be completely enlightened, in an unbreakable state of bliss. Then my spirit can conquer the defilements of ego and relative comparison.* He remembered something his Aikido instructor once said to him after class: *Sensei told me, "A soul is both clarified and invigorated when two kinds of saltwater meet ten thousand gallons of fresh water." Why did he speak to me in a riddle? What does it mean?*

Noticing a deck of playing cards on a table below the framed calligraphy, Jack recalled an invaluable life lesson taught to him by his father. He vividly remembered the day when he was fourteen years old that his father taught him the game of blackjack. After teaching the rules and dealing a few hands, his father shared an unforgettable insight with him.

Dad taught me something of importance, Jack recollected. *He took a break from teaching me the literal game of blackjack, and spoke of a figurative, applied blackjack. He told me, "If the ace of diamonds is the only card in your hand, you'll indeed be dealt a queen. This could at first appear to be a victorious pair. However, the queen will forever be facedown. You will never know what suits her, diamonds or a loving heart. Try to embody the ace of hearts, become a master in the ways of affection. Once an aura of benevolence surrounds you, many queens will present themselves.*

If you can become an ace of hearts, each girl will be transparent like a watch crystal. Softly grasp her small hand with your big hand, then sense if she speeds up or slows down. Break your connection with her if she fails to stay synchronized with you. If she accelerates, she needs to control you. If she falls behind, she needs you to control her. If she keeps pace with you, she is in search of a relationship based on mutual trust and understanding—a balanced relationship which bears the dual luxuries of passion and companionship. Together, an ace and a queen of hearts share a twenty-one year old spirit as long as they live. If you lose your way, just remember the clockwork of blackjack."

Soon after that memory passed, Jack's friend Rodney called from the city of Jacksonville in northern Florida:

"Hello?"

"What's up, Jack? It's Rod."

"What's up, buddy?" Jack asked. "How've you been?"

"Well, my girlfriend and I are gonna walk down the aisle," Rod responded.

"Congratulations, I think, but I know you don't mean that aisle so feared by fraternity guys like yourself!" said Jack.

"That very one," Rod reassured him.

"I remember a time when the three of us had a few drinks at a bar in Tallahassee. I figured you two would get engaged before long. You and she always seemed to have that chemistry, but it's still a surprise."

"Well, Jack, I guess I've found the one."

"Life has dealt you some good cards, bud, there's no doubt about that."

"That makes me think we should get a poker game on," said Rod.

"Yeah, we should do that as soon as I get back to F.S.U., back into your neck of the woods."

"I'll be visiting a couple of my fraternity brothers in Tallahassee pretty soon. We'll get a card game together and play some golf, the two most expensive pastimes in existence."

"Alright Rod," Jack concluded, "I'll call you when I get back to Tally. I'll have my rusty golf clubs, a deck of cards, and a half gallon of bourbon ready."

"Ha-ha, sounds like a formula for success to me. Take it easy, and I'll see you in a few weeks."

Jack hung up the phone, and went into the kitchen for a glass of lemonade. He and Rod went to different high schools in Miami, but they knew each other from playing on their schools' golf teams. Rod had recently graduated from F.S.U., for he was a year older and a grade ahead of Jack. Rod and his girlfriend had already been "engaged-to-be-engaged" when they decided to move to Jacksonville. About a two and a half hour drive from Tallahassee, Jacksonville was one of the places where Rod had been offered a job, and it was the city in which his girlfriend's parents lived. He was in a fraternity, unlike Jack, but they were nonetheless like brothers. They shot pool, played golf, and were known to turn up at the notorious bars on Tallahassee's Kentucky Street from time to time.

Rod and Jack could hardly stop laughing when they remembered the hilarious antics of some people they knew. They sometimes played golf with a middle-aged Englishman named Arthur who called everyone "mate". He always shouted expletives after hitting a shot. There was something unusually entertaining about his combination of accent and word choice. No matter how good his shot, he would curse the golfing gods and throw his club either down the fairway or into nearby trees, at which point Rod and Jack would duck for cover. Remembering this character gave Jack a good laugh: *I guess he never read the book Golf is Not a Game of Perfect.*

Laughter lasted for a while, but these times could not be relived. Rod was one of many of Jack's friends whose path had swerved one way while his veered another. The memories could not replace the people, and although ten thousand had gone away before 10,001 would be no easier.

There will be a bachelor party I'm sure, Jackson thought. *Soon after that, Rod will be legally joined with either his perfect partner or his ball-and-chain, or perhaps a survivable mix of the two. Nah, this one is a keeper...she'll be a great wife. I can't wait to find the one who matches my pace, but rash pursuit will lead only to heartache. I must be patient and keep my eyes open...look for ones with whom I can blend smoothly. I'll consider the reasons for my current lack of a love life tomorrow. Right now, I need some sleep.*

Ready to retire for the night, Jack undressed and climbed into bed.

A couple of hours after he fell asleep, his eyes began moving rapidly in every direction. A vision slowly formed in his brain: he was standing in the desert, near the Great Pyramids at Giza, Egypt. He was the only person in sight, and he was gazing at the tallest pyramid.

Without disturbing a single grain of sand, the sky tore open. A gargantuan male hand adorned by a Star of David shaped ring reached down from the sky and unscrewed the apex off the largest pyramid. Then it did the same to the other two pyramids. The hand then squeezed all three points together, crushing them and scattering their sands across the desert.

Jack awoke at that moment, and recollected the dream vividly. He asked himself silently, *Is there some great meaning to this vision? Or was that simply my mind up to its common midnight tricks? It sure seems like something more...* He drifted back to sleep, and did not awaken again until noon.

Cognitive Dissonance

"A man who has never experienced cognitive dissonance has always followed his heart, but he will one day realize that his brain is better suited for leadership."
 ^ *from* the short story *What Guides Us?* by Jackson Muldoone

    Jack awoke the next day and cooked eggs and toast for breakfast. Then he drank a glass of orange juice and returned to his room. The news of Rod's engagement had affected him. Jack was glad for his friend, and he perceived a heightened potential for success in his own future relationships. However, he then wondered why he was without a girlfriend. *It seems I have not yet aced the matters of the heart*, he thought.
    Jack went to his bedroom and turned on his CD player then turned off the light and sat Indian-style on a thick couch cushion. It was time for reminiscence. He placed a dip of wintergreen-flavored smokeless tobacco between his gum and lower lip to speed his thoughts. As the burning in his gums increased, so did his rate of processing information. *Nicotine*, he thought...*a highly addictive poison that makes parts of me work better. With all the health risks, though, I'd better give it up someday.*

Soon to join with his past, he risked having to weather an emotional firestorm. However, Jack felt that walking through a battlefield was a small price for what he was compelled to do—he had to upset a thousand grains of sand to search for crucial answers. His favorite vehicle of introspection and retrospection was piecing together an imaginary autobiography. His vision of thousands of people someday reading his life-story instilled him with focus and a greater sense of purpose. He mentally "wrote" about the things of importance to him, and foremost was the fairer sex.

Jack had been fond of a number of girls in his life. Before college he had crushes, but he rarely dated and tried to live within the less turbulent worlds of sports, friends, and music. At any rate, this was a time for Jack to think back to the times after high school graduation, when he first began to form enjoyable intimate relationships. *I took pleasure in each one of them*, he realized, *yet each attachment dissolved. I'd love for any one of them to be by my side right now. I'm going to put the pieces together…listening to the music of "Enigma" will help me solve this puzzle.*

As the result of either striking coincidence or Jack's subconscious orchestrations, the song "Morphing thru Time" began playing from the stereo. *I guess that's my cue*, he thought, *If I can elude the enemy— those toxic neurological connections—I'll manage to return unscathed.*

Ok…the summer after high school…I had the summer off since I wouldn't be going to West Point. Why didn't I go there? So much tradition and beauty at the military academies…so much honor and unparalleled intensity. I could be parachuting or flying a helicopter right now…why aren't I? Ah, that's right, my self-doubt told me I couldn't wake up at 0500 hours. In addition, I feared having 25 hours of work to do each day. Most importantly, at the military academy I wouldn't have found time for a love life, something I was eager to acquire soon. This may have been West Point's blessing in disguise after all…no time for a relationship means no time for a heartbreak.

I had chosen not to do what I believed would make me in many ways a better person. As a consequence of my conflicted decision, my beliefs

on what was best for me had changed noticeably, theref
of my actions. Why am I on this tangent? I'm suppo
contemplating my past relationships and the obstacles that kept
of them from developing.

Jack's thoughts began to focus on a girl he had dated during his summer before college—the tall, thin, and undeniably beautiful Karissa. The first memory to surface in Jack's mind was her voice. *She spoke so softly with that high-pitched voice,* he thought. *She carried herself so gently, never raising her voice or making exaggerated gestures. If only she didn't have two years of high school left at the time, we might've lasted a long while.*

Our relationship never became serious, because we realized we'd be living five hundred miles apart as soon as I got to college. As beautiful as she was, I might have fallen victim to "out of sight, out of mind." I'd have been far from her eyes, and she would've been far from mine. Who knows, though, maybe absence would have made our hearts grow fonder.

Suddenly, a sense of longing, frustration, and surrender struck Jack all at once, like lightning, an earthquake, and a tornado all converging on a tumbleweed, which was once roaming casually with the breeze, then hurled haphazardly in every direction without its consent, hoping only to find comfort once more. "Chloe," Jack whispered. Then he thought, *I could write a sequel to The Odyssey about her. She's worthy of ten thousand epic similes and her very existence proclaims divine intervention. It would take ten thousand stock epithets to encompass her character.* Jack's memories of her were the most vivid—the most stinging. *I've arrived at one of those poisonous memory banks,* he thought. *This one I can't dodge. I'll have to remember everything, from the beginning...*

I was inside Moore Auditorium on campus, waiting for social psychology class to begin. A thirst must've found me, 'cause I remember walking outside toward the vending machines. A petite brunette was already at the soda machine, considering her options and about to make a purchase. I looked at her legs and gluteus muscles to consider her options. If she were an automobile, she'd be a Lotus

Esprit Turbo with a top-of-the-line custom bumper. Each of the blond streaks in her hair would be a racing stripe.

Jack's silent laughter about the car analogy kept his spirits high while he brought back this overwhelming memory, like a coal miner riding into an ominous tunnel, similar to a tunnel in the brain, might joke with his colleagues, not completely relieved by the cheerful conversation, but absorbed in it enough to keep the otherwise engulfing fear of entrapment at bay.

What was going through my head next back then? Ah yes...I noticed her tight blue jeans and white tube shirt. A jealous Harley Davidson leather jacket found itself gripped in her right hand. Ha, she probably knew how to ride a motorcycle...scary. From the back she looked perfect, but I wanted to get a glimpse of her from the more significant angles. She bought her drink and went inside the auditorium. She was still "face-down", but I remember noticing her enticingly energetic walk.

Now that my curiosity was running high, I sat down in the auditorium and looked around for her. After casually scanning all the distant seats, I found her one row behind me, and a few seats to the right. A mighty jolt coursed through me, and a complete hollowness followed suit. At that moment, I realized how many pieces were missing in my life's puzzle, and I knew exactly where each of those pieces could be found—contained within this girl just out of reach.

She was beyond comprehension. It seemed more like I was watching a movie than perceiving real events. Is this a normal phenomenon in social psychology? Her face was the ultimate combination of adorable, innocent, and arousing. Her skin was a satin finished shade of creamed espresso. Her hair was brown with those perfectly placed blond streaks. She had full breasts and ideal proportions. This girl, this woman, this incredible bipedal creature, was composed of every physical attribute a guy could dream about. Her looks were only half the equation, though, as her personality and lifestyle would in turn have to be assessed.

My thoughts became Olympic sprinters on a track with no finish line. I sought some fundamental information, wondering—how can I approach her? Why did it take me half a semester to notice this celestial body? Does she have a boyfriend? If she notices me, will my appearance inspire a double take? Will I ever walk around campus with her riding upon my shoulders? It wasn't yet time for forming extreme goals such as this, I realized, but it was surely time to ask her to join me for a dance.

I would have to approach without approaching, invite without inviting, and hope for her acceptance to a proposition never proposed. If she in fact wanted to dance, I'd have to flow without music, touch only with words, and keep my spirit-mind in tune with hers. If only I'd begun Aikido before then, I'd have had a far better understanding of blending and "ki-no-musubi"—the connection of energies. The damnable misery of it was that I'd only had one chance to succeed in those proving grounds of the auditorium. I'd never before entered the playing field when the stakes were so high. They'd never been so high.

The class only met once a week, and the next six days were painfully mundane. Being in the proximity of such a premium young woman, then spending days nowhere near her was like living contentedly eating hamburgers and French fries each night for dinner, then for a month partaking of the most tender chateaubriand and lobster tail, accompanied by the finest red wine, only to abruptly revert to fast food which then seems unworthy of even the family dog's consumption.

Friday arrived again and I subtly peered around class as I walked through the doorway. She wasn't there. I sat down next to my friend Kara and conversed with her until class began. Maybe she'll walk in late, I thought. She didn't show. I had seen her face, but I still couldn't tell if she was a materialistic queen of diamonds or a kissable queen of hearts. I had to remain objective—I couldn't make the mistake of assuming that sparks were flying for her just because they were for me. After all, she might be like an exquisite ice sculpture of an eagle, chiseled to aesthetic flawlessness, while full and untouchable within, and unable to turn her head to view the wings she possesses, thereby unaware of her potential to soar beyond the worries of the world. If only I could've shown her wings to her, inspiring her to trade the easy satisfaction of complacency for adventure and discovery.

Once the class was over, I walked with Kara back to our dorm. There would only be two more classes—two more opportunities to dance with that sensual and adorable mystery girl. In every other scenario I can recall, for me to actually start thinking about a girl when she wasn't in my presence, she had been in my presence several times beforehand.

Fearing there was too little time for a passionate flame to be ignited, my mind methodically dissolved its fantasies of her. This must have been a defense mechanism—I had felt harsh disappointment before. That next week was good...I'm sure I thought about her much less. I talked with friends on the front porch of the dorm about the three fundamental topics—music, sex, and movies. I had polished off another week of college, and I walked toward the auditorium for social psychology class.

I entered the auditorium and failed to notice any of my friends inside. I did, however, notice the dream girl sitting alone. Despite my forfeiture of the fantasy of becoming close to her, I walked down her row and sat two seats away. A tingle shot through my spine, delivering all the recently subdued fantasies back to my conscious mind. That natural high was intense and surreal, like driving a motorcycle at high speed, at the break of dawn, and in a dense fog. I had to make a move that seemed natural, at the right time and in the proper context.

At the end of class, the teachers handed out attendance cards, and we filled in our names and student identification numbers. Once we filled them out, we were told to pass them to the left. Perhaps this is my only chance, I thought. She was sitting on my right, and she handed her card to me. I read her name off the card and said, "Hi, Chloe, I'm Jack." I briefly analyzed her name and found it smooth and sophisticated.

"Hi," she responded "You're the first person to ever pronounce my name right on the first try."

A lie no doubt, but a lie that made me feel like a king. "Good to meet you," I said, reaching a hand toward her.

She shook my hand and smiled, exposing perfect teeth and a pair of irresistible "hug-me" dimples. That was it, I was in love. Class was over so I left, mumbling a few words to her before we went our separate ways. What did I say to her? Must've been some meaningless small talk. I had hoped it didn't sound stupid. Some of the ice between us had melted, but we had made only an initial connection on a trivial level. I had yet to invite her to dance. I thought I might get the chance at the next week's final class, but only time would tell.

During the next week, I remember socializing with friends and new acquaintances. One day, I walked past Robby's room and heard, "Jack, are you up for a little basketball?" That certainly sounded like a good idea. I changed my shoes and we began the mile long hike to the gym. Robby had a girlfriend he'd been with for quite some time, but he nonetheless was a man who understood what worked in beginning new relationships. I asked him, "Robby, there's this girl who I'm basically in love with, though some would call it infatuation, and all I know about her is her name."

"So you're whipped, then?"

"I don't think so," I said. "If I were, I'd be at home in the fetal position listening to love songs. The problem is I get this crippling lightheadedness when I'm around her, and I know I can't say what I need to say."

"I've known that feeling," Robby empathized. "Just say something to her that half-way makes sense. You'll be more likely to punch yourself if you never try than if you bravely shoot a three-pointer and she rejects it back to half court."

"She's only about five feet tall, so her shot-blocking ability is dubious," I replied, "but as I'm releasing the ball, she could kick me square between the legs."

"That's just the chance you've gotta take," Robby said with a laugh, probably feeling like a motivational speaker. "Try to stay on the same team with her if you can, don't be a ball-hog, and remember you're playing full-court."

I always liked people who weren't afraid to speak in metaphors from time to time. That sort of conversation brings new and often-humorous associations to otherwise isolated topics. Those intense games of basketball always had a mild cleansing effect on my system.

A small, predictable cycle would take place—endorphins flooded in as my fears sweated out, leaving me in a state of mild euphoria. After each game, I'd glide in autopilot toward the nearest water fountain.

Back to Chloe now. Where did I make my mistakes? Ok, on the way to our final class, I realized that it would be my last chance to get to know her. I knew that if I walked in and sat next to her, a panther would claw my tongue, leaving me mute and uncomfortable for that whole hour and a half. I wouldn't have had one sliver of confidence, because I wouldn't have known if she had any interest in me. In that scenario I could be talking and exchanging smiles with her, only to hear her ring the death knell: "My boyfriend loves that movie..." or something along those terrifying lines. So, we would have to sit next to each other, of course. But I couldn't sit next to her. The only solution was to arrive at class early, then sit one seat from the aisle. There was a slim chance that—if she was interested in me—she'd take the empty seat at my side. That would give me the confidence I needed—the confidence to shoot the game deciding three-pointer at the buzzer.

I went into the auditorium and sat next to an open aisle seat. It was then or never. Two things could happen. In all likelihood, she'd sit somewhere else and remain a beautiful mystery forever. In the snowball's-chance-near-her-body event that she sat next to me, I'd be in that wonderful, near delusional state at least until the end of class. When the teacher began lecturing, there was still no sign of her. There appeared to be an unthinkable third scenario—the one where she decided to skip class. At the exact instant in which I thought I'd never see her again, the door opened and she came through the threshold.

Forsaking three hundred other seats, she walked straight toward me. I remember thinking how fantasies like this had never come to fruition for me before, and I was extremely uncomfortable realizing this one was about to. There must've been some sincerity behind her smile when I had introduced myself to her the week before, because she sat down quickly in her reserved seat.

She was a black hole, and I had no choice but to be pulled into her depths. I smiled at her and asked, "Chloe, right?" as if her name hadn't run through my mind a hundred times since I'd learned it. I couldn't let her know too soon that she was the most attractive girl I'd ever seen, 'cause in this mangled upside-down world her interest in me would've diminished. She said, "You remembered!" I then asked her if she remembered my name, only to bring about a puzzled look on her face. My words to her from the previous week appeared to have soaked in like water into a duck's back. I told her my name was Jack, and she responded with a playful pseudo-paranoia.

She said, "How do I know that's really your name?"

I responded, "Can't you take it on faith?"

Then she looked at the essay I was holding and saw the name "Jackson Muldoone" on the top.

"So why was your essay written by some 'Jackson' guy?" she interrogated.

"It would almost appear to the keen-eyed observer as though I have a nickname, then, wouldn't it?" It was fun speaking with her in cynical, quasi-condescending tones, and it kept me from appearing too love-struck.

She giggled, indicating the conclusion of the name-game. I loved her playful energy, partly because it helped me stay comfortable. She was even carrying a Barbie doll which had come with her McDonald's happy meal, but she nonetheless seemed mature, displaying only a healthy type of silliness. Had there been needles protruding from the doll, however, a door would've opened into an entirely different area of speculation. After an hour and a half of small talk, I was sure all the signs were there. I knew I had no choice but to ask her if she wanted to go somewhere with me, and I held my breath while I searched for the right words. Unfortunately, my car was back here in Miami that semester. Due to that fact, the difficulty in asking her out increased tenfold.

"Does Barbie wanna play some pool?"

"I don't know, you'll have to ask her," she replied. At that point I possessed the highest level of nervousness possible, and loss of consciousness was imminent. A dizzy spell was coursing through my body.

"Hey Barbie," I inquired, forcing myself not to stutter, "wanna shoot some pool?"

"Ok," responded Barbie while dancing on my leg.

I told Chloe I didn't have a car, and she said she'd drive. We began walking to her car, and I wanted so badly to sweep her up and carry her all the way. I was too shaken up by the recent series of events to know what type of actions might charm her, so I stayed as conventional as possible. My casual speaking style had deserted me, and I must've made a dozen out-of-character remarks. Why couldn't I be myself around her? I knew that would be the only way it could've worked. I guess it was hard to stay in reality when reality had never been so generous with me. We arrived at Penelope's Pocket and shot pool. She had more ability than most guys, which both impressed and discomforted me simultaneously. I was hoping she'd exhibit some weakness—some sign that she wasn't already perfect without me.

Our night ended without a sufficient attachment developing. I loved being near her, but I couldn't decide if she was a girl whom I could trust. I had only played half-court; so I could always tell myself, "it didn't work out because I didn't really try." It must've been an ego-defense thing. It had all seemed too good to be true. As a result, I only made a half-assed effort to build common ground between us.

The next day, she was leaving town for a week. She gave me her number but I never called. I saw her again only in a handful of scattered dreams. To keep from feeling I'd missed a chance, I envisioned her having an unattractive personality, even though deep down I considered her a good person. I began to think that she was an emotionless egomaniac. I envisioned her getting enjoyment out of manipulating others...even her own friends. Maybe she liked to deceive people by shaping their emotions—by making every remark and facial gesture with a premeditated and devious purpose. Doing this might have empowered her with twisted feelings of superiority and control. She definitely seemed smart enough to toy with people. Perhaps endless flattery and admiration, even from men of low persuasion, had instilled her with arrogance—an unacceptable, self-destructive conceit. Maybe if she were my girlfriend, she'd secretly have a long-distance boyfriend back in her hometown.

Perhaps she'd had to reject ten thousand guys in the past, feeling guilty the first few times, but—with each occurrence—she had become increasingly numb, like perpetual drips of liquid nitrogen fed intravenously on a path to her heart, methodically freezing her feelings of guilt and self-blame while collaterally deadening every other emotion notwithstanding two hundred degrees below zero.

What prevented me the most from pursuing her, though, was simply my belief that she wouldn't feel the same overwhelming intoxication around me that I'd feel around her. In spite of all my unsubstantiated derision of her personality, I'd have married her in a hummingbird's heartbeat.

Chloe wasn't the only girl I've considered marrying, just the only one I've felt I could have after merely one look. Am I really that reckless in considering prospective life-long partners? It was probably a safe thought, being as how the odds that she and I will ever even kiss are slimmer than the odds of winning the jackpot on a slot machine while Tiger Woods simultaneously scores a bogey. I would've been willing to spend a lifetime with Jen, but I had seen far more than just her face before I came to that conclusion. I had also seen her personality, and—ah yes—her naked body. Most memories of Jen are pleasant ones.

Tanqueray Jenna Davies, whom I most often called Jen, was born and raised in a small town near Montpelier, Vermont. Her father owned a local general store, and she worked with him when she had free time. I met Jen and her roommate through our mutual friend Kara, and dated Jen's roommate for a month or so. When I finally concluded that Jen's roommate was not quite what I was looking for in a girl, I considered the unthinkable scenario—the "roommate switch". I knew I had to make a perfect golf swing to make that happen. Everything would have to come together in the right way, and at the right time. Much to my amazement, it did.

The first month was full of passion and companionship, topped off with a five-day trip to Archipelago Adventures Theme Park. However, our relationship during the second and final month became purely sexual. Although our physical gravity was intense, the emotional ties between us were dissolving. The final closure to our relationship came that day when I saw her walking alone, and she looked at me for a second then looked away. Her face was expressionless and apathetic. Could I have tried to get things back to the way they were between us? Certainly, but at what cost? She had still meant a lot to me, but at least there were no more maybes.

If I could only be in a meadow right now, lying on a blanket with either Chloe, Jen, or Karissa—kissing any one of them, or perhaps all three, inhaling those opiates which fill the air in love's proximity.

Jack looked over at his clock, which displayed 9:00pm. He could hardly believe that he had spent seven hours contemplating his past. Although he felt an acute emptiness in his head, he was glad that his memories did not drag him far down into the dumps. Then he realized that the nugget of smokeless tobacco, which he had placed in his mouth seven hours ago, still remained. *I got my money's worth out of that wad*, he thought with a smile. He went to the bathroom, washed it down the sink, and swooshed some tap water through his mouth. His belly felt as hollow as a hot air balloon, so he walked to the kitchen and made himself a TV dinner in the microwave. It was his favorite two-minute meal, baked chicken with mashed potatoes. He inhaled the food and chugged a glass of apple juice before returning to his room.

Back in his lair, a familiar song grasped Jack's attention. The lyrics reassured him that others sometimes felt emptiness within. He felt an overall sense of forfeiture, resulting from memories of people entering his life only to exit abruptly and indefinitely.

He began to sing along passionately, wishing that everyone he missed could relate to the longing in his voice—

"But someday we'll meet again
And I'll ask you
I'll ask you why

Just tell me why
Why it has to be like this,
That the good ones disappear
I'm asking you why"

Jack stepped onto the patio and sat by the swimming pool. He lit a cigarette and began searching for resolution. *Why do the good ones disappear? He* asked himself. *Should I have gone to West Point after all? Would I have been better off in that world without enough time for dating? Is dating a losing-man's game? Are the pains truly inseparable from the pleasures?*

He knew he wouldn't find the answers to these questions unless he could calm his spirit-mind and return to the source. *Must be ten thousand forces pulling us in different directions,* he thought. *There are so many variables, so many events taking place beyond my influence. Pyramids...Egypt...Star of David...apexes removed...crushed to sand. I may never understand that dream. I need to gather a spirit of tranquility and hold an ace of hearts in my hand.*

Two luminescent green dots passed slowly in front of his face. He was startled at first, but then he realized what it was. *I forgot about those lantern click beetles,* he thought. *I used to call them glow bugs when I was a kid. Amazing how they emit that brilliant green light. They turn their tiny lamps on and off erratically it seems...maybe sometimes they want to be seen and other times they want to blend with the night. I'm heading back to school tomorrow, so maybe I'll get in a meditation now. Nothing sets my mind at ease like spending an hour alone, in absence of thought.*

Sushi Sympathy

"Should carnivorous men and women feel ashamed for eating animals? Does the lioness live in shame for devouring a gazelle?"
^ *from* the short story *Delicious Guilt* by Jackson Muldoone

Jackson drove 500 miles from Miami to Tallahassee, returning to his two-bedroom apartment for another semester of college. He was considerably more enthusiastic about Aikido and girls than business classes, but success in all three ranks would surely not displease him. It was time for him to adapt once again to a place demanding decisions and independence.

It was a Wednesday afternoon, and the new semester of school had not yet begun. There was an Aikido class scheduled for that night, so Jack began preparing for it. The first thing he did was open his weapons bag and remove his jo—a five-foot wooden staff designed to resemble the spear once wielded by ancient samurai. Though it lacked a blade, the jo was clearly formidable in its own right. He was walking out the door with it when his roommate, Paco, said, "What's that for? Are you going hiking?"

"No, it's a practice weapon for that martial art I told you about," Jack responded.

"Oh, it's for that akita then?"

"No, it's much too heavy for a dog to fetch, it's for EYE-KEY-DOE."

"Oye, just don't break one of my bones with that thing if I leave some dishes strewn about the apartment, o.k.?" Paco said jokingly.

"Have no fear, Buck-o, Aikido is the martial art of peace."

"Mira, that's one of the most oxymoronic contradictions I've ever heard. Now, in the least literal sense, take that broomstick and go break a leg at your class. Tell me more about this uhkito someday."

"Alright, enjoy watching the rest of that 'Miercoles Gigante' game show. I watch it sometimes myself, because the girls are sexy and their foreign tongue lets me pretend they're speaking—um—indecently."

Paco said goodbye then continued watching the television show. He had gone to high school with Jack and they had been good friends ever since twelfth grade. Paco's parents were born in Cuba and managed to flee Castro's regime with the help of Hermanos al Rescate. Paco was about as straight-edged as they came; he never smoked or drank alcohol, and the only drug he was fond of was caffeine.

Jack arrived at the dojo, the Aikido practice hall, twenty minutes before class. He sat next to the only other student on the mat—a girl named Kimberly who was casually stretching her muscles. She was a fair-skinned redhead with long legs and a relatively short torso. Jack had gotten to know her a bit, and he developed a peculiar fondness for her dark sense of humor and sharp-edged wit. He turned to her and said, "I'm glad you're here early; I hate being the only one in the dojo."

"Well, I try to spend as much time around you as possible," Kimberly responded with every sarcastic tone she could muster.

"Yeah, I can have that sort of effect on people," countered Jack. "Do you want to get some sushi after class?"

"Sure, I'll get some seaweed salad and tempura vegetables," she said.

"So you're afraid of eating raw fish, then?" asked Jack.

"No, actually I'm a vegan. For both spiritual and nutritional reasons, I don't eat animal products."

My curiosity has been piqued, Jack thought. *She's one of those soy milk junkies. I'll enjoy learning her reasons for such an eccentric diet.* They both began silent pre-Aikido meditation while other students and the sensei walked into the dojo. The sensei clapped his hands then kneeled in the center of the mat, signaling the beginning of class. *Sensei*, Jack thought, *Japanese for "teacher". Everyone should be both a student and a sensei in his or her own right.*

The first technique that the sensei demonstrated left an imprint on Jack's mind like no other had before. For that technique, the sensei called Jack to the front of the class to play the role of attacker in the scenario. Both Jack and the sensei were armed with wooden swords. As soon as the sensei lowered his weapon, Jack thrust his sword, aiming between the sensei's ribs. At the last second, the sensei stepped off the line of attack and countered with a swift cut that instantaneously separated the air above Jack's head. The sword only missed by a fraction of an inch. *Sensei is truly a master*, Jack thought. *He's a master of timing and adjustment.* After an hour and a half of exercising various throws, joint locks, and pins, Jack and Kimberly both felt invigorated and hungry. They made their final bows to the other students, to the sensei, and to the mounted portrait of O'Sensei, the "Great Teacher" and Founder of Aikido.

Kimberly and Jack left the dojo, almost side-by-side. Kimberly discretely quickened her pace and began walking a half step in front of Jack. *She sped up,* Jack noticed, *so perhaps she wants to be in control...I'll name the restaurant and see how she responds.*

"Takeshi's Wasabi is my favorite sushi restaurant," Jack proclaimed. "Let's go there."

"I prefer Musashi's," Kimberly replied, "but Takeshi's will be fine." Jack detected a bittersweet tone in Kimberly's voice, with a slight emphasis on the bitter.

"Takeshi's it is, then," Jack persisted. "Their seaweed salad is greener and more flavorful, just so you know."

"I see," said Kimberly, "but I might have to sacrifice my morals tonight."

"How's that?" asked Jack excitedly.

"I'm not sure if vegetables can satiate my hunger. I might have to eat some sushi. I'm so hungry I could eat a carelessly sliced poison blowfish."

"They don't serve puffer at Takeshi's," Jack replied, "which is probably for the best. Besides, I trust you wouldn't throw away all your morals on account of a little hunger, would you?"

"Of course not, it was just a hyperbole for effect."

They rendezvoused with Bessy then set off for Takeshi's Wasabi. On the road, Kimberly and Jack conversed about their favorite musical artists and Aikido techniques. Kimberly's hair glided over her left shoulder as she sharply turned to peer out her window. Jack glanced at her and could hardly believe what he saw; more specifically, he could not believe what he had not seen before. The shifting of Kimberly's hair revealed a silver dollar sized tattoo of a black spider centered on the back of her neck.

"How long have you had that?" Jack asked as he touched her tattoo with his forefinger.

"I've had it for a couple years now. Do you like it?"

It's morbid and creepy, Jack thought, *bordering on terrifying*. "It's a bit shocking at first, but it certainly—um—adds character."

"It's a black widow," Kimberly informed him.

"How inviting," he responded. His cynical tone was resounding. "Don't black widows have a red hourglass-shaped mark on the abdomen?"

"They certainly do, but it would've cost an extra $50 for that marking."

"Time is money, as they say," he said in a clever tone.

She replied with a half-smile, "You know why they call this spider a black widow, right?"

"Actually I do," he said, feeling the mild pride of knowing. "The female black widow bites and kills the male immediately after they mate. It would seem that cuddling is not high on her list of priorities."

"That's right," Kimberly said. "The male makes the ultimate sacrifice. He procreates then provides food for the future mother. If only humans were this advanced, this efficient."

"Let me stop you right there, before you begin to frighten me. Besides, there's the restaurant."

The red hourglass, he thought. *Such an ominous symbol. The black widow reminds us that even if her poison fangs don't catch us—time will.*

Jack parked his car and walked beside Kimberly toward the front door. Just before arriving at the entrance, Kimberly accelerated and opened the door for him. *There she goes again*, he thought, *maybe she believes in some sort of reverse chivalry. At any rate, I could never have a girlfriend who wears the pants in a relationship. That would leave me donning the skirt...completely unacceptable.* In that moment, he realized he would not want more than a friendship with the garnet-haired vegetarian before him.

Jack recognized the host on duty at the front podium. It was Takeshi, the owner, manager, host, and occasional bartender of his quaint Japanese restaurant.

"Onegai shimasu, Take-san," said Jack with a bow.

"Domo arigato gozaimashita, Jack-san," replied Takeshi. "Thank you for coming to my humble sushi bar once again."

"This is my friend Kimberly. She usually eats at Musashi's, but I'm helping to expand her horizons."

Kimberly offered Jack a playful stare, then said to Takeshi, "I'm looking forward to the seaweed salad. I hear it's the best in town."

Jack interdicted, "Actually, I let her know that it's the best anywhere, from America to Nippon."

"Ah, Jack-san, you are my number one business promoter. A complementary bottle of sake for you and the lady tonight!"

"Many thanks," Jack replied.

Takeshi showed them to their table and told them about the night's sushi special.

"Tonight we have delicious unagi, which is grilled freshwater eel. I'm offering it at a special price of two for two dollars. It's my personal favorite and I highly recommend it. Your waitress will be with you in a moment. I hope you enjoy your meal."

Takeshi returned to his hosting station, while Jack and Kimberly kneeled on silk cushions at the dining table. A petite woman dressed elegantly in loose-fitting, silken attire walked softly towards their table. Jack noticed her hair; it was smooth, glossy, and jet-black. A solitary chopstick held her hair in a doughnut shape behind her head. Jack silently considered the waitress's aesthetics: *so tasteful, so clean, so refined*.

"Takeshi said to bring you this," the waitress spoke softly as she set down a large ceramic bottle of rice wine with two small cups. "Our host is a gracious and generous one."

"Thank you," Jack responded. "Kim, are you ready to order?"

"Yes," she said to the waitress, "I'll have the seaweed salad and tempura vegetables please."

"I'll also have the seaweed salad," Jack said, "as well as four pieces of unagi and the teriyaki chicken."

The waitress finished writing the order and said, "It'll be just a few minutes."

"So Kimberly," Jack began to ask, "why is it you don't eat animal products?"

"Animals can have diseases and unhealthy chemicals in them. Also, I'm opposed to the way animals are kept. They live in terrible conditions just so people can be happy with their meat, eggs, and milk."

"I understand your point of view," Jack replied, "because I think about that myself from time to time. I guess I'll never know what it feels like to be a cow or a chicken, so I assume they don't suffer much. The other assumption, and the one you seem to make, is that animals do endure pain and suffering in their living conditions. If I didn't enjoy meat and other animal products so much, I would probably give animals the benefit of the doubt as you do. I assure myself that animals are not people, and cannot see their own death. This helps me sleep at night, and I don't feel guilty for my animal consumption."

"That's why most people consume animal products, and we vegans are in the minority. Like you said, we give animals the benefit of the doubt. I used to be addicted to meat, much as you seem to be, but then I learned about the inhumane ways in which animals are sometimes kept. I may never shake my newfound abhorrence for meat."

"Well, they may be treated in inhumane ways, but don't forget that they are inhuman," Jack said lightheartedly. "I hope my chicken doesn't make you nauseous when it arrives."

"No, it won't. Watching others indulge themselves doesn't make me sick. Remember, I used to eat it myself. Then I realized that chickens have souls too, you know."

Jack nodded once then filled the two cups with sake. He then proposed a toast: "To chicken souls."

"Cheers," Kimberly said, offering her two cents worth, and they partook of their potent potables.

In-between sips of Takeshi's signature sake, Jack glanced around the restaurant. He noticed a few groups of fellow diners then a painting on the wall of a woman holding a fan. She wore whiter-than-snow makeup and was peering down towards the fan at her chest. Jack gazed and noticed a mountain painted amidst Japanese writing on her fan. *Must be Mount Fuji,* he thought. *I've seen pictures of that mountain. It's a substantial landmark to the Japanese. Perhaps the woman is protecting the mountain—guarding some secret it possesses.*

"Isn't that a thought provoking painting over there?" Jack asked Kimberly, pointing towards it.

"I guess so," said Kimberly. "Looks like all that makeup feels hot on her face, so she's cooling off with the fan."

"Maybe that's all there is to it," said Jack, "but for some reason I think there may be more."

Before any more commentary could be made on the painting, along came the waitress bearing a colorful array of edibles.

"Enjoy," said the waitress, "and remember, Takeshi's world famous blue wasabi is hot enough to forge steel. I recommend you use it sparingly, and with respect."

"Thank you," Jack told the waitress, "but don't worry about me, Miss, I like my sushi without a horseradish inferno."

Both Kimberly and the waitress chuckled, then the waitress walked toward another table.

"You look a little preoccupied, Jack," Kimberly said with a grin.

"I was just thinking about some things, nothing of importance. How's the seaweed salad?"

"You were right," Kimberly conceded, "it *is* better than Musashi's."

She's willing to admit she's wrong, Jack thought. *Perhaps she's only a semi control freak. I've already made up my mind though, we'll be friends and hang out together, but a romance is out of the question.*

"So, Kimberly, now that we're becoming friends, tell me a little about yourself."

"Let's see. I was born in Lisbon, Portugal. My mom is Portuguese and my dad is the captain of a U.S. Navy cruiser. He's American, of Italian and Andorran descent. He's at sea six months of the year, which kinda sucks. When he's back home in Maryland I spend as much time with him as I can; he's a great dad. I moved to the U.S. before I was two, so I don't remember much about Europe. My mom has a nice array of photos from Lisbon, though. The city looks absolutely beautiful in those pictures."

"All that sounds pretty amazing," Jack said. "Do you have any addictions? Caffeine and nicotine have a firm grip on me. I'm hoping to find one day an Aikido technique that can separate me from their grasp. I obviously drink, but only every now and then."

"I smoke weed sometimes," Kimberly replied, "but I'm only a recreational user."

"Well, at least you're still sane then. When you begin to think you smoke weed to somehow heal or even save the world, you've past the point of no return."

"Ha-ha-ha," Kimberly burst out laughing. "I know the stuff is poison, but, as if my head is a mindless empty shell, I do it anyway. I used to do other drugs, at a time in my life when I was chasing the ultimate high."

Beginning to grow sickened of the drug discussion, Jack decided to change the subject: "How are the vegetables? I've never had them here."

"The batter is crispy and the veggies are fresh," Kimberly replied. "That's the winning combination."

"That's two out of three," Jack said, "but why don't you try the tempura sauce?"

"Don't you know it's made from fish stock?" Kimberly responded. "You wouldn't want me to taint my beliefs, would you?"

"Whoa, I didn't realize the scope of exclusions to your diet. You must truly be serious about this stuff."

"*I am most serious!*" snapped Kimberly.

Jack looked towards the bar and spotted the perfect conversation piece. A red-handied samurai sword lay resting within a blue scabbard on a wooden stand.

"That's Takeshi's favorite katana over there," Jack said while pointing. "From what I hear, swords are the symbols most revered by the Japanese."

"What fascinates them about it?" Kimberly asked. "It just seems like a long, curvy razor."

"Well, it takes a precision craftsman many long hours to create it. He hammers and folds the steel until it's sharp enough to make a razor seem like a butter knife. The construction of the intricate hilt and handle also takes time and patience. My favorite aspects of that sword are the Japanese character for fire on the handle and the tsunami emblem on the sheath."

"I like the color scheme of it," Kimberly added.

Red and blue, Jack thought. *Flame meets a tidal wave. Yin blends with yang. Fight fire with fire? No, envelop fire with water until all conflict has been flushed away. That is Aikido.*

As they finished their food and drink, Takeshi walked over to the table.

"How is everything?" Takeshi asked with a smile.

"It's delicious," Kimberly responded. "There's such a pleasant atmosphere in your restaurant—a radiant ambience."

"We were just conversing about your sword at the bar," Jack said. "It brings an edge of authenticity to the place." To clarify that his pun was unintentional, Jack considered saying "so to speak" but realized that would only make matters worse.

"Ah yes," replied Takeshi. "I named her Crimson Tide after the nickname of my alma mater, the University of Alabama. Some say that if you mix fire and water with base matter, you can turn it into gold."

Surely he doesn't believe in alchemy, Jack thought. *Though perhaps there's a spiritual message hidden in his words. Turn dull thoughts into glittering golden ones?*

Jack temporarily stopped his analysis of Take's comment and said to the good host, "I can't believe I never noticed that painting before—the one of the woman and the fan."

"That painting has been in my family for two centuries," replied Take. "It's my favorite piece of artwork."

"Is that Mount Fuji painted on the woman's fan?" asked Jack. "And what do those four calligraphy markings around it mean?"

"Yup, that's Fujiyama. The writing is four words: heal, inspire, grow, and haiku."

Haiku... Jack thought... *at first glance simple, yet in truth a most sophisticated vehicle for expression...my favorite type of poem...no room in a haiku for detailed description...a reader must see between the lines...fill in the gaps to paint his or her own picture.*

"Isn't Fuji a volcano?" Kimberly asked Take.

"Yes, but it hasn't erupted in almost 300 years. The crater is sealed, and some tourist shops have been built there. I hope to climb it one day." Takeshi's smile persisted, reflecting his enthusiasm for conversations pertaining to his homeland. "I hope you both will join me again soon here in my humble restaurant. Jack-san, keep your studies your first priority, and remember—while a little sake refreshes, too much hinders the brain."

"Thanks for the words of wisdom, Take-san. I'll leave my money here for the waitress," Jack said as he paid for both his and Kimberly's meals, including a twenty-percent gratuity. "Sayonara, Takeshi."

"Don't say sayonara, Jack-san. That means goodbye forever. When your palette is once again ready to tame our menu, I shall see you then."

"See you then, Take," Jack said as he and Kimberly rose to their feet.

"See ya," Kimberly followed.

Takeshi offered a deep bow towards the two of them in gratitude and respect then walked toward the bar to help other customers.

"I'm glad we did it," said Kimberly to Jack. "This restaurant exceeded my expectations, and I do prefer it over Musashi's. I had less sake than you, so should I drive back?"

As they walked out the door, Jack replied, "I only had about one beer's worth. I'm well under the legal limit. Besides, Bessy gets a bit irritated when an unfamiliar driver takes the wheel." Jack immediately followed his comment with a smart-assed smile.

"Funny," Kimberly replied as she climbed into the passenger seat.

Jack started his car and left the parking lot of Takeshi's Wasabi. After some small talk with Kimberly, he dropped her off at her apartment. Before she left the car, Jack offered her his fist. She also made a fist, and then she ritualistically tapped both ends of his fist with hers. Jack and Kimberly were both fond of this form of friendship gesture, known as "daps". *Now she knows I just want to be friends*, Jack thought. *The discomfort of uncertainty is gone.*

"I'll see you Friday at Aikido," Jack said to her as she climbed the stairs leading to her apartment. After watching her go inside, he pulled open the plastic wrapper of a fortune cookie that he had saved from the restaurant. He broke open the cookie, ate it, and then he read the hidden message. *Your character can be described as natural and unrestrained.*

Civil Disobedience

"Mediocrity's complacent sands must be disturbed."
^ *from* the short story *Ego and Complacency* by Jackson Muldoone

Jack parked outside his apartment and looked at his watch as he climbed the stairs. *Some say that time is the most important thing*, he thought. *It's 10:24pm. I have plenty of time for a meditation.* He walked through the door to his apartment and saw his roommate Paco, who was dressed to go out.

"Are you headed out?" Jack asked.

"Yeah, I'm going to Rocky's Saloon with a couple of my boys. I'm hoping to find a gorgeous, somewhat inebriated female who'll say, 'Take me drunk I'm home!' Bro, where have you been?"

"I went over to Takeshi's for some sushi with this girl from Aikido."

"Oh, now I know why you do that uhkito. It's a nest full of ladies."

"Buck-o, you know I have a passion for the martial art, and this lady's just a friend."

"A friend with benefits?" Paco asked, grinning.

"No, although I wouldn't mind if she were. Good luck finding your drunken soul mate tonight at Rocky's."

"Thanks bro, I'll see you tomorrow when I get home from some girl's house."

"Yeah, later."

Paco left the apartment and Jack found himself alone. *Now I can have a full, undisturbed meditation*, he thought. He placed his John Coltrane CD into the stereo and listened to the song "Blue Train". *Good ol' Rick*, he thought, *my old roommate who introduced me to jazz. What ever happened to him? Why do the good ones disappear? There's something untainted about jazz. I wish I could've met John Coltrane*...Jack ceased his thinking for a moment and just listened. After the music refreshed him, Jack decided it was time for meditating

Pyramids—Egypt—Star of David—apexes removed—crushed to sand, he thought. *Will I ever understand that dream?* He stopped the CD player and opened a book entitled *The Secrets of Aikido*, then he rehearsed the "four gratitudes". After re-reading and remembering the four directions of thanksgiving, Jack placed the book back upon the shelf and reached for a lighter and an incense stick. Clutching the lighter and incense in one hand, he used his free hand to pour uncooked rice into a small green bowl. He then stuck the incense into the bowl of rice and lit it while whispering, "May the scent of burning sandalwood cleanse my mind of all defilement."

Jack then lit the first of four candles that were placed in the corners of his room. He whispered softly, "My gratitude toward the universe, the source of all life." He then lit the second candle, whispering, "My gratitude toward nature, the provider of our daily sustenance." Finally, he lit the third and fourth candles, whispering towards each, respectively, "My gratitude toward my ancestors and parents, who are responsible for my personal existence," and, "My gratitude toward those other human beings who make society flourish. May the Light of peace and truth, Kami no hikari, shine upon us all."

After lighting the candles, Jack sat cross-legged on his bed and gazed upon a small statue of Buddha in a corner of his room. One of the four candles burned just in front of the statue, thus casting a shadow of Buddha's head and long, drooping ears upon the wall.

He thought, *Siddhartha Gautama Buddha, and all others who have* sacrificed high status and exorbitant riches in the pursuit of purity and truth, thank you for your inspiration. In today's world one can be rich both spiritually and financially, but only if money is earned honorably. You gave so much to this world, Buddha, you are one of the great teachers. There are and have been many like you...many great teachers...many buddhas.

Unfortunately, I fear that many would-be buddhas have found it difficult to attain enlightenment in today's world. I wish to join these heroes who heal and provide medicine for our ailing world, yet something hinders their enlightenment. It's as if a thin fog—a translucent haze—surrounds their bodies. It's not nearly as thick as the opaque cloud encapsulating the ignorant ones, but it's enough to keep away perfect transparency and prevent their ascension into buddha-hood.

I must find ways to dissipate the cloud that engulfs me, but I can't achieve complete peace of mind if I must live in a world of turmoil. Maybe that's why so many others never let the cloud vanish...maybe that's why some have become monks, to live in environments conducive to happiness. There've been many good people in my life who possess only the thinnest of fogs, but most of these old friends and teachers have disappeared. Why do they disappear?

I've got to unify with a woman one of these days. Without her I'm only half of what I could be. When will I meet my soul mate? Chloe—I thought you might be the one. Perhaps what they say is true, that fate can only set the stage, and then we must play our own roles. You played your part, but I failed to play mine. Where are you now? Why did you disappear? Perhaps one day there'll be another stage set for us, and I'll not buckle under the pressure like I did a few moons—no—a few dozen moons ago. You took my heart and made it disappear before I could even notice. Did you put it in your purse? Do you carry it with you always? Do you wash your hands while you break from playing with it? I placed it in your hand, hoping for an even exchange, but you made it disappear. Your skill is high in sleight of hand. If only you had my address, you could mail me your heart in the form of three words or *so. Since that seems too much to hope for, I suppose all I can do right now is try to empty my mind and return to the source.*

Powerful emotions filled Jack with stress, so he took a deep breath. Then he used the back of his hand to wipe gathering sweat beads off his forehead. He managed to begin letting his thoughts flow through, hoping that all thinking would cease, so he could pass into the elusive realm of no-mindedness. He had learned he could not accomplish this through forced thought suppression but rather by permitting each thought to run its course until it faded away.

A painful, neutral, or pleasant thought alike must run its course, he pondered, *like an incurable virus whose cycle is often vicious, sometimes innocuous, and all-too-seldom beneficial.* Jack found he could achieve a true "no-mind" only on rare occasions, and—after twenty minutes of perpetual thinking—it seemed to him that once again "no-mind" would elude him.

This'll be a thinking meditation, he thought with a silent sigh of acceptance. *These can often be dangerous. Sensei once cautioned me as to the power of meditation when he said, "Some thoughts which had been better off subdued will re-surface. However, much progress can be made during those vulnerable moments." He also once told me, "A soul is both clarified and invigorated where two kinds of saltwater meet ten thousand gallons of fresh water." What was he referring to? He must've thought I'd understand that riddle someday, or he wouldn't have shared it with me. Fresh water meets salt water—an estuary? Which estuary? Two kinds of saltwater? Perhaps one day the answer to that riddle will sneak up and surprise me, but any further contemplation of it seems fruitless.*

Jackson enjoyed a few minutes of mental clarity until his memory of the pyramid dream re-surfaced. *Peaks of the pyramids removed*, he thought, *by a hand donning a Star-of-David ring—the hand of a Jew perhaps.* Then another vision formed in his mind, and this time he was awake. With his eyes closed, suddenly he could see Washington, D.C. He was inside a structure, looking out a window. He turned to notice a total of eight windows, two on each side.

I've been here before, he thought, *I'm in the Washington*

Monument. I'm at the top of this grand obelisk, looking out over our nation's capital.

He remembered visiting D.C. with his school in eighth grade. He had brought an old penny, which he had soaked in Coca-Cola to remove its tarnish. When his group got to the Lincoln Memorial, he had left the penny in Honest Abe's hand, whispering quietly, "One cent, one sense, one love." Jack had always been eccentric.

As that memory passed, he found himself still in the peak of the Washington Monument. He stretched out his arms, and pictured himself placing his hands on the two imaginary windows in front of him. He bowed his head and whispered, "universe." He turned ninety degrees on his bed and again envisioned his hands on two new windows. With another bow he whispered, "nature." Then he turned again, and in the same form he whispered, "ancestors." He turned one last time and whispered, "human beings." Without warning, the monument began to shake. The pyramid-shaped apex of the building began to lift from its foundation.

Jack was now in the open, exposed. He envisioned the crest of the monument brought into an enormous, yet effeminate hand. It was the hand of a black woman. The fingernails were painted cobalt blue. A woman's body to control the hand was nowhere to be seen. It squeezed the tip of the monument until white dust fell to the ground steadily as sand through an hourglass. The hand then opened and came near to where Jack was standing. Its fingers curled inward then extended a few times, beckoning Jack to come closer. He jumped onto the hand and it gradually lowered him onto the grass.

Jack opened his eyes and thought, *she didn't want to harm me. She just wanted to help me...learn something...but what? Blacks and Jews were enslaved at times in history. They are two different ethnic groups sharing terrible similarities. Perhaps—out of vengeance—they want to destroy the monuments of their oppressors. For the Jews who were enslaved in Egypt—the Pyramids. For the Blacks who were enslaved in America—the Washington Monument. But in my visions these hands didn't destroy the structures, they only lifted off the tops and crushed them...there must be something more here, some deep symbolism. I learned in history class that George Washington was at least kind to his slaves, and he set them free in his later years. The hand in D.C. wasn't there to kill or take revenge. Neither was the hand in Egypt. No maliciousness—no hatred—no vendetta. Why then? Is there something more for me to gather from these visions? Could be...*

Jack opened his eyes and noticed that the tea candle in front of his Buddha statue was fading. He took the candle out of its holder and noticed that it was out of wax. He moistened his thumb and forefinger with his tongue and pinched the dim glow that remained. Then he found a replacement candle in his drawer. He put the new candle into the holder and pushed it slightly closer to the metallic Buddha. He struck a wooden match and lit the wick, reciting, "My gratitude toward other human beings who make society flourish."

After watching Buddha's shadow flicker on the wall for a few seconds, he glanced at the clock, which read 12:21am. Knowing he would have a class the next morning, he set the alarm for 10:00am. He turned the alarm clock face down so that no light would emanate from it. Then he went to the corners of his room and blew out all four candles. The only remaining light was symbolized in the framed Japanese calligraphy hanging on the wall behind his bed.

Jack touched the smooth, protective glass that enclosed the character hikari. It was too dark for him to see the ink, yet he extended his second and third fingers and traced the ancient symbol flawlessly. Without a sound, he mouthed the words, "Hikari...Light...may the Light of the universe illuminate everything and guide us along that Smoothest Flow. May it conduct our grand orchestra. May the Light pass through me and everyone else as it does this glass frame." Jack's head felt strained. A single tear rained down his cheek, but it failed to rinse the pain. He thought, *I've got to somehow wash away my internal conflicts soon.* He studied the author's drawings in the book *Aikido and the Harmony of Nature.* Then he felt a little better. He got under his sheets and drifted away.

Cascading Catharsis

"When passion is lost and confusion plagues the brain, suppressed emotion must be released to cleanse the spirit."
^ *from* the short story *Feeling Again* by Jackson Muldoone

Jackson awoke the next day to his chiming alarm clock at 10:00am. Feeling depressed and having no desire to arise from bed, he pressed the snooze button and slept until 10:09. He went through the snoozing process three more times until he finally got out of bed at 10:36. He walked onto the porch and lit a cigarette. *I've got class at 11:00*, he thought. *I've still got time for my morning coffee and a quick shower.* He finished his cigarette and made a cup of instant coffee in the kitchen. He noticed that the coffee had not filled the mug, and he thought, *There's still room.* He reached into the pantry and pulled out a bottle of Irish Cream Liqueur. *My Irish ancestors have concocted a most delicious coffee creamer*, he thought as he poured about an ounce into his mug. Jack chugged the mildly spiked coffee then exhaled with an "Ahhh." He made a beeline for his shower, turned on the water, and began to shampoo his hair.

While the water fell over him from the showerhead, he remembered a drawing in the book *The Secrets of Aikido*. The drawing consisted of a man undergoing waterfall misogi, a spiritual cleansing ceremony, which was practiced frequently in the Far East. He conjured up the idea that standing under a waterfall might be just the fix he needed. *I've gotta find out where I can do waterfall misogi around here,* he thought. *Maybe that can soothe my aching brain. Perhaps the heavy, tumbling waters of nature can extinguish these fiery conflicts within.*

Jack hurriedly got dressed and walked outside, not surprised to see Bessy waiting for him. *Bessy,* he silently spoke to his car, *if only the rest of the world and I could be more like you...so dependable...so capable...so altruistic...so smooth. All you ever ask for is 87 octane. On your birthdays I spoil you with 93.* He drove to class and read 11:03 off his watch as he walked through the door. He found an open seat on the right side of the classroom, thinking, *Professor, I hope you don't find me disrespectful for being late. I need my morning coffee.* After sitting down, the professor began to speak. He said, "Welcome to Business Law three-thousand. I'm Dr. Parnevik and we'll be learning all about the legal environment of business."

What am I doing in these business classes? Jack asked himself. *They bore me to tears. I should be studying astronomy or Japanese calligraphy instead. I must be in the bottom chamber of the hourglass sometimes, foregoing passion for the pursuit of money and ego.* He glanced around the room casually. He did not see any familiar faces among the twenty-person class, but he took notice of a couple females whom he wished were familiar. *Well, so far I see a handful of pretty girls and two absolute hotties,* he thought. *I can't complain. I'll have to make an educated guess as to which one would be best for me, and I'll sit next to her tomorrow.* He discretely began studying the two "hotties" for a few minutes while the professor presented the course outline. Not knowing their names, he decided to think of them as "Potential-1" and "Potential-2." *One day, life will teach me not to go after the prettiest ones,* he thought, *but I haven't learned that yet.*

Potential-1 sat in the front row at the far left of the classroom. Jack first noticed her complexion, which appeared flawless and had an olive tone. *Here's an exotic one,* he thought. He studied her thin, straight, light brown hair while avoiding direct eye contact. He did not want to get busted. Though careful as he was, she turned her head suddenly and caught him looking at her. He subdued his initial instinct of looking away, and gazed at her with a soft expression on his face. Potential-1 smiled at him then shifted her attention back to the professor. Jack's heart quickened its pace and his jaw lowered a half-inch.

She glows, he thought. *I've never seen a face radiate more raw beauty, and her upper body appears streamlined, but she doesn't have the overpowering glow that emanated from Chloe. Chloe's aura was fueled by both spiritual and sexual energy while this girl's is only sexual. I get the feeling that this girl would be the best sex I'd ever have, but she might never cook for me, give me a back rub, nor help me find peace of mind. It's a definite plus that she smiled at me, but was there a true smile within her smile? Either way, I'm already becoming infatuated with her.*

To keep himself from getting too attached too soon, Jack turned his focus towards Potential-2. She was sitting next to another girl in the center of the class, one row in front of him. He took notice of her wavy blond hair. Then she turned her head to speak with her friend, exposing her face to Jack. He saw her eyes, they were jade green and attractively large. *I wish I could read lips*, he thought, *so I could learn something about her. She's sitting with her friend...she doesn't feel alone, which might make it tougher for me to get to know her. She might be content with her friend's company and therefore not in need of mine. It's settled, then, I'll sit by Potential-1 at the next class.*

Class ended and Jack drove back to his apartment. He walked through the door and saw Paco, who was busy in the kitchen.

"What are you up to, Buck-o?" Jack asked, greeting his roommate. "Making espresso?"

"No Jack, like I've told you before, espresso is just dirty water compared to this. I'm making café Cubano and cooking some hamburgers for lunch. I'm brushing up on my cooking skills for when Taija comes over for dinner tonight."

"Who's Taija?" asked Jack.

"I met her last night at Rocky's near the bar. I bought her a screwdriver, got her digits, and invited her over here for dinner tonight."

"So you're gonna cook for her? Isn't that a little risky?"

"Not if I were fixin' burgers, but I'm gonna impress her and make veal parmigiana. I've never cooked that before, so it will be dangerous indeed. Jack, this girl's drop-dead gorgeous; I've gotta go all-out. I'll cook you a piece of veal too. When you see her, you might want to worm her away from me. Pero I'm not worried. She'll have one taste of my cooking and be mine forever!"

"If she lives up to her sexy name, I might be jealous. Taija—it kinda just rolls right off the tongue." Jack went to the refrigerator and poured himself a glass of orange juice while Paco placed a hamburger onto a bun. Jack drank the sweet, tangy juice then walked into his bedroom and turned on his computer. He said to Paco, who was out of sight, "I'm gonna take a nap in a minute, but I'll be around to meet your date. We'll see if she's as gorgeous as you say."

"See you in a little while, bro," replied Paco. "Trust me on this; it's impossible to exaggerate how hot this girl is."

Jack started his computer and went on-line. He began surfing the Internet for nearby waterfalls, out of a curiosity inspired by his whim in the shower that morning. He typed three words, "Waterfall-Florida-Georgia," then he clicked the search button. After a few seconds, his computer responded with 10,283 returns. He clicked the first search return, which was summarized as "Falls of the High Noon Sun State Park—Alythop, GA," and a new screen displayed. Jack scanned the web page with accelerating eyes. He moved his lips silently as he read the location information.

Alythop, GA? I've never heard of that city. According to the map, it's only a hundred and ten miles from here. Bessy could get me there in an hour and a half. I could go there right now and be back in time for Paco's gourmet cooking. I'm gonna do this. The place looks perfect in this picture...nature in all her purity.

Jack took a towel off the hanging-rod in his shower, and then he grabbed his wallet and keys. He printed the map from the park's web site then glided through the living room and kitchen. He was a man on

48

a mission. As he walked out the door he told Paco, "I'm going to Georgia to stand under a waterfall, but I'll be back for the veal and what other tender young meat might be present."

Jack stood in the threshold as Paco responded with a subtle snap in his voice. "I know you'll treat her with respect as soon as you see her, so I'll just pretend I didn't hear that. If you're going for a ride in your car to listen to music, you can just say so. You don't have to conjure up imaginary little adventures."

Jack laughed as he closed the door, assuring himself that his joke about Taija did not offend his love-inflamed roommate. With fresh hope, he walked to his car and studied the direction map in his hand. As he started the engine, he spoke aloud, "Well Bessy, looks like we're taking I-75 all the way to Alythop." Then he thought, *Oh God, I'm talking out loud to my car...I hope I'm not truly losing my mind. It might take more than a couple hours with nature and some falling waters to salve my wounds...but it seems worth a try.*

He put his "Invisible Man" CD into the player and headed for Interstate 75. Bessy's stereo system blared one of Jack's favorite songs, "Samurai," by Michael Cretu—

"Your commission was written in the sand
No emotion could ever stay your hand
No consolation
No word of love or praise
Your fight is over
Your enemies are gone
Your fight is over"

Listening to his favorite music, driving at high speed, and embarking upon a great adventure, Jack could already begin to feel an emancipation of his soul. He still felt a bit depressed and confused, though, and he could hardly wait for nature's healing hands to be laid upon him.

His focus turned toward an eighteen-wheeled truck on his left, which he was slowly passing. A spark of immaturity overtook him, so he stuck his arm out the window and pulled his fist down then pushed it back up several times, hoping that the truck driver would see. Knowing the honk-signal all-too-well, the driver was a good sport and pulled his truck's air horn twice. *It's a bond of camaraderie*, Jack thought, *two men on solitary missions sharing a moment of truth.* Smiling from ear to ear, he passed the truck and looked up to the sky, unable to find even a single cloud. He did notice a flock of buzzards high and to his left, and he thought, *perhaps a bad omen, but at least they're not circling right above me.*

Jackson exited the interstate then saw a sign that stated, "Welcome to Alythop / Pop. 337." He had been driving for an hour and a half, and he had listened to two compact discs in their entireties. Replete with excitement and anxiety, he smoked a cigarette as he navigated the small town. He saw a gas station, and he was about to stop for directions when he suddenly noticed a green sign on the roadside: "Falls of the High Noon Sun State Park / next left then 3.5 miles." *It's 2:30*, he thought, *I hope they don't turn the water off after high noon.* Joking with himself kept Jack comfortable in the face of being in another state, more than a hundred miles from home, and all alone.

Before making the turn to the waterfall, he noticed a restaurant called *The Greasy Spoon Gourmet* adjacent to the gas station. Although the diner's name fed doubt into his brain, his stomach remained hungry. *That must be the only place in town for lunch*, he thought, *so I suppose I'd better stop there. I just hope they don't charge me ten dollars for "gourmet" grits and hash browns.*

After he parked Bessy in front of the restaurant, Jack walked along a concrete path toward the front door. A sign on a post told him to seat himself, so he did. There were two other people in the building: a cook and a waitress, both donning gold caps and blue-and-red striped aprons over gray shirts.

"Good afternoon to ya," the waitress greeted Jack. "My name's Christina, just holler when you're ready to order. The menus are sticking up right behind the ketchup on the edge of yer table."

"Ok thanks," Jack responded as he reached for a menu.

The prices are reasonable after all, he thought. *Looks like breakfast is served all day. Maybe I'll try those hash browns, along with some eggs, bacon, toast and coffee.* He looked at the cook, who was cleaning the grill. *Such mundane jobs these two have, he thought, but they appear completely satisfied. Maybe I could learn a thing or two from them.* Jack raised his hand and the waitress came over displaying a warm smile.

"What can ah get foh ya?" she asked.

"I'd like the Ultimate Grease Breakfast Combo, please."

"How would ya like yer eggs, darlin'?"

"Over-hard, please."

"And ta drink?"

"I'd like a glass of water and a cup of coffee with cream and sugar."

"It'll just be a sec, hun," she concluded with a comforting tone of voice.

He watched her give the order slip to the cook, and then he put a dollar in the jukebox and selected three songs. The songs he chose had one thing in common—an upbeat, free-spirited melody. This was neither the time nor the place for angry or depressing music. He managed to find one of his favorite songs on the jukebox, so he played that one first. It was "Doing the Unstuck" by *The Cure*.

He sat back down and watched the cook prepare his meal, noticing his blue and red apron. *Blue and red*, he thought, *just like Takeshi's samurai sword. Fire and water...yin and yang. The gold cap! A symbol of enlightenment, which reminds me of what Takeshi was saying at the sushi restaurant...with a proper blending of fire and water, one can produce gold! Maybe fate brought me to this restaurant...there is much to learn here. Some day, I'll write a short story entitled "Beyond Coincidence" about these times when enough specifics come together to make a grander scheme appear likely.*

"Order's up, Christina," the cook hollered energetically. The waitress brought Jack his food, coffee, and water then returned to her seat at the counter. Although the food looked delicious, Jack was a bit disappointed that it was not greasier. *I guess the meal's name built it up so much that I couldn't be anything but let down. This restaurant must not be quite the grease-monger it makes itself out to be.*

He poured cream and sugar into his coffee, then chugged it almost in one gulp, saving the water to wash down his food. He ate every bite of his meal except a small piece of bacon fat. He had learned it was impolite to clean his plate completely, although he did not know the purpose of that particular social grace. He left enough money to cover the check plus a twenty-percent gratuity. As he walked toward the exit, he said, "Have a good day" to the cook and waitress.

"Bye, hun, thanks for stoppin' by!" said the waitress with a bubbly smile.

"Don't be a stranger, now," said the cook with a wave.

As he walked toward Bessy, Jack lit a cigarette and reflected on his lunch. *What a wholesome meal and such friendly service…I hope the rest of my day goes this smoothly.* Bessy took him down the road en route to the State Park. They arrived at a gate and Jack paid three dollars to the park ranger for entrance. He then drove to an empty parking lot. As he got out of the car, he grabbed his "Go for the Gold" beach towel and his wooden Aikido staff. Before walking away, he gave his Probe a quick look. *Bessy,* he thought, *you're such a dark, dark blue…you look so sad right now…are you?* Knowing that Bessy would not telepathically answer, Jack turned and noticed a signpost with a colorful map pasted on it. He read the map, studying the one-mile nature trail leading to the waterfall. *I'm glad I brought my jo…it'll make a perfect walking stick.*

Jackson began his journey down the trail, highly enthusiastic about getting to the falls. He could see many types of trees and ferns, some of which had labels on signs stuck in the pine-needle-covered dirt along the trail's edges. Remaining alert to avoid copperheads or other venomous snakes that might cross his path, he hiked onward, often uphill and occasionally down. He used his makeshift walking stick to clear out a few unavoidable spider webs. After hiking for fifteen minutes, he was intrigued by an oddly shaped rock on the side of the trail. The rock was about the size of a basketball, and it was adorned by fossil imprints: some twisty and others fan-shaped.

Jack set down his jo, crouched, and overturned the rock. A small spider was on the underside, and it crawled into a hole. As the spider hid, Jack saw a bright red hourglass mark on its abdomen. He dropped the rock and jumped back, feeling his heart rate double. *A black widow...it could've bitten me and I'd be out here all alone to die. I'd best be more cautious in these woods...the cheerful birdsong seems to belie hidden peril.* He resumed his march until he came upon the waterfall. *Here it is,* he thought, *even more beautiful than in the picture on the web-site. Falls of the High Noon Sun—such a fitting name...the waterfall is surrounded by trees...the sun can only be seen from this tiny, circular clearing at midday. This is an awesome place.*

Jack took off his sandals and sat on the water's edge. He put his feet into the water then immediately pulled them out. "Ooo, that's cold!" he cried out. *I came all this way,* he thought, *and I'll be damned if a little nip in the water is gonna faze me!* He again lowered his feet into the water and looked around, observing the cell of pure nature in which he was enclosed.

The only human touch to mar this place was a wooden sign that warned, "SWIM AT YOUR OWN RISK." Though it instilled some fear in Jack, the sign made the whole experience seem all the more intense and adventurous. He listened to the sound of the waterfall; it was a continuous "shh." The sheets of falling water fell from a small creek above. The creek continued downhill and there was a somewhat circular swimming hole in-between. Into this small reservoir the falls poured.

Jack unclothed except for his swim trunks, and he thought, *I hope I don't get hypothermia.* He slowly submerged into the collection pool and swam toward the falling layers of crystalline liquid. He pictured his sweat, which had coated his body during the hike, wash downstream. This only partially refreshed his spirit, however, and he gazed all around in search of something that might bring him peace.

He found that he could stand, as the water was but four feet deep. He could also swim, and he was grateful to have both options. Not yet ready to brave the roaring falls, he floated in the fetal position for several minutes while his body slowly adjusted to its bone-chilling new environment. While he was curled up on the water surface, some of the confusing thoughts that had been plaguing him returned.

These visions, he thought, *one waking and the other in slumber. Enormous hands tearing off the tops of monuments, crushing them to sand with the tightness of their grip. Robby, Chloe, Jen, Karissa, and all my other old friends and teachers...all of you who have helped me better myself...why have you disappeared? Do the good ones always disappear? Mom, Dad, Kimberly, Rod, Paco, Sensei...one day we will no longer be able to share with each other. Will everyone I've ever loved soon disappear?*

Jack walked under the waterfall and turned to face downstream; he was chest-deep as he stood. The water was heavy and thick, and it pounded the top of his head as if someone from above was emptying numberless buckets of ice cubes. He started crying as a consequence of both physical and emotional discomfort. He cried for five minutes while the culmination of his so-long-submersed mental turmoil presented itself.

Tears cried out of loneliness joined the clear, tumbling stream, until Jack suddenly opened his eyes wide and began laughing hysterically. It was as if the water had shorted a faulty circuit in his brain. *Of course,* he began to piece things together. *My sweat and my tears—two types of saltwater meet ten thousand gallons of freshwater! Waterfall misogi is the meaning of Sensei's riddle!*

Feeling instantly healed, Jack took a step behind the falls and peered through the water's lens at blurry trees in the distance. He was in a meditative trance, and his soul had become pure light and energy. *I will never know why the good ones disappear, but I know that I am a good one, and I've oftentimes disappeared myself. Good ones meet other good ones, all throughout our lives. Some enter as others leave, and we share as much as we can, while we can. Bringing some form of aid to others while keeping a pro-social big picture in mind is what makes us good ones. We are all born in the upper chamber of the hourglass, all good ones.*

However, temptation is a fisherman with a wide array of lures. Going for the bait will bring us below, not to an inescapable hell where evil reigns, but to a world without peace...a world without love or respect. Sometimes I've been drawn into the bottom chamber, and I've felt the power of ego, but now I truly understand why feeling proud, strong, or important in that underworld is a delusion. To live in the chamber beneath is to be caught in the web of relative comparison. It is to become trapped by unnecessary fears, which block the potential to live in the Flow. One who doesn't escape becomes food for the black widow.

Jack felt a small fish nibbling on his calf muscle, so he gently shook his leg. *I'll be damned if a little nip in the water is gonna faze me*, he thought for the second time, smiling freely at the dual meaning. *I'd strip down to my birthday suit, but these fish might mistake something more sensitive than my leg for food.*

Then he analyzed the visions of the Pyramids and Washington Monument, for the first time with a pristine spirit. *If we are in the bottom chamber long enough, we become satisfied with who we are and the way everything's going. Through an ultimate act of compassion, a human being might disrupt another's sealed mind, to take away his or her thoughts of completion. Only after ego is shattered can a once-ignorant bottom-dweller begin to learn and grow, to rise up to the better world—the world of the good ones. Then that person will be no longer ignorant of his or her inherent perfection. That's what the visions represent. An upper-dweller, who is entirely free of hatred, must partially enter the bottom chamber in order to rescue a bottom-dweller. This is a perilous task that requires ultimate bravery and determination in both the savior and the saved.*

I feel as though some immense energy has transformed my spiritual sands in the Hour Glass into part of the surrounding glass itself. I no longer feel as though the wind tosses me about the world. Instead, the wind moves around me and through me as I breathe. My body still weighs two hundred pounds but my spirit once again floats softly in the grand scheme...the Light guides me in the Smoothest Flow. If I can stay as transparent as glass, I'll be able to see through anything, and anything will be able to see through me. If I can stay clear, I'll no longer hide the person I am, and I'll no longer fear. When one has a conscience but no fear, one lives in the Flow.

I'll expect nothing and blend to the best of my ability with whatever occurs, whenever it occurs. I'll help others find the energy to transform their spiritual grains of sand into glass, where they can join all the enlightened ones and never be lonely. Happiness can only be attained in the upper chamber.

Jack swam through the waterfall and floated on his back in the middle of the collection pool. He felt renewed, like he was a different person than the one who made his journey to the waterfall. His new self felt strangely familiar to him, and it did not take him long to come to grips with who he had become. He had the same brain with which he came, but the waterfall had been a catalyst in cleansing his soul.

Of course! He thought. Enlightenment isn't about gaining something new…it's our restoration of what we all were given at birth! Twenty years worth of the dirt and debris of emotional conflict had been sent downstream, and his spirit was identical to the one that filled him as a child. His faithful trust in the grand scheme returned. His knowledge and mental abilities as a young adult merged with his freshly invigorated spirit, and this brought him back into the Flow, only now, unlike in his childhood, he was ready to understand.

Jack remembered his roommate's offer to cook him veal parmigiana. Though it had not been long since lunch, he was hungry again and wanted to meet Paco's new lady friend. *I still have needs and desires,* he thought. *I learned in social psychology class about Abraham Maslow's hierarchy of needs, and I've believed in it ever since. There are a few aspects of his model that I feel could be revised…perhaps I'll humbly modify it a little.* He remembered the pyramid as this:

Self-Actualization
Self Esteem
Love
Safety
Physiological (Food, Water)

Then he remodeled it in his mind:

Self-Actualization
True Self Esteem
Love
Moral Action
Safety
Physiological (Food, Water)

I've moved some of the pyramid's stones around, he thought. *In each model, an upper-level need cannot be satisfied until the one below it has been. We can never be fully self-actualized, though, as there is always room for improvement. One who is in the self-actualization stage can erupt like a benevolent volcano, spreading wisdom across the world.*

True self-esteem comes without relative comparison. Thinking something like, "I'm better than he is, so that makes me good," is too easy. We must only gain esteem by comparing our present selves with our past selves. In doing so, we can improve continuously and not rely upon basing our success on what appears to be failure in others. The need for moral action must precede the need for love. Moral action is not synonymous with legal action although the two often coincide. We must not take action with a wonton disregard toward consequences that might hurt others. When one acts immorally, one acts antisocially...a sociopath cannot feel love.

This place has changed me, freed me...I hope I can retain this clarity of mind forever. I'd better get home now.

Jack got out of the water and noticed that he was not having convulsions. *My body must've adjusted to the cold...I'll be physically numb for a while.* He picked up his towel and used it to dry off, then he wrapped it around his waist. He put on his shirt and rubber sandals then reached down for his jo. After taking a final glance back toward the waterfall, he hiked down the path. A translucent snakeskin caught his eye in the nearby woods. He picked it up and studied it for a moment then placed it back down and smiled. *A copperhead shed this,* he thought. *Now it's a gold-head. I need to get out of these wet shorts as soon as I get home.* The trail ended, and he rendezvoused with Bessy.

Before climbing into his car, Jack noticed a small, green leaflet between the windshield and the wiper, and he was baffled and appalled by what he saw written on it. It exclaimed, "JOIN US for the monthly meeting of Klan Chapter 149, featuring guest speaker Grand Dragon Simon Pauerlust of Ku Klux Klan Southeast Brotherhood!"

Jackson suddenly felt an overwhelming sense of duty: *I should go to this place and bring my Aikido weapons, both mental and material, and use them to inoculate each and every one of them, methodically destroying the disease to which they are host. They'd see my blond hair and blue eyes and welcome me with open, white-enrobed arms to their perverted powwow…then I could catch them unawares.*

Every person has a need to feel important, that he or she is part of something. However, when not acknowledging the underlying perfection of all people, one's sense of self-significance is delusional and must be dissolved. Those in hate groups are bottom-dwellers, feeling satisfied in the chamber beneath. They are antisocial miscreants who poison young and old minds alike, perpetuating racism's vicious cycle like blind mice scurrying along the wheel of degeneration. Fear of another race's racism begets racism. To hate is to be hated, which further fuels hate's fire. Only by rediscovering our inner water can we douse this fire. This destructive wheel must be reinvented.

These people need power over others to keep them from feeling weak. They are like malicious, razor-toothed angler fish, lurking in those deepest of depths, below the reach of the Light's glorious finger, so—instead of accepting the challenge of swimming up—they create their own artificial light, which they use to attract their prey, smaller fish that might have one day chosen to surface, but now these small fish stay down because they have been seized by a mesmerizing and more readily available light on a bigger fish with sharper teeth.

I cannot save them by myself, however, for they would surely harm someone who would threaten their comfortable, albeit illusory world. I must keep close to heart my favorite of O'Sensei's songs, which is the cornerstone of Aikido philosophy—

"One who, in any situation
Perceives the truth with resignation
Would never need to draw his sword in haste"

Jack crumpled the leaflet in his hand, then pitched it into a nearby trash can. He stood away from Bessy and engaged in jo kata: defense and attack forms with his wooden staff. He swung it through the air, this way and that, and then he blocked and thrashed against an imaginary, yet all-too-real, white-hooded foe. After taking a deep breath, he sat inside his Probe and headed home.

He listened to the sound of the wind while watching passing cars. *I wonder how many of the passing drivers are going to that "brotherly bonfire,"* he thought. *Probably no more than a few, but that's a few too many.* Despite these and some other saddening thoughts, he managed to keep a peaceful mind for most of the way home.

Arriving at his apartment at dusk, Jack opened the door and saw a woman with shining strands of light brown hair sitting at the candlelit dinner table, but he could not see her face. He could see Paco's face, though, sitting across from Taija.

"Jack," Paco said, "I'd like you to meet Taija."

Taija turned to face him. She was Potential-1!

"Nice to meet you," she said, recognizing him from class.

"You too," Jack responded, partially frozen, "I think we have a class together."

"Yeah, Business Law, right?"

"Yeah, I think that's the one. I've been swimming, so I've gotta change out of my wet clothes. It's nice meeting you."

"Jack," Paco re-entered the conversation, "there's a piece of veal in the kitchen for you whenever you get hungry."

Jack went to his room, undressed, then put a dry towel around his waist and lay down in bed. *It's times like this when the grand scheme's twisted unpredictability used to disturb me severely,* he thought. *But because I'm not attached to her, and because there are ten thousand Potentials with whom a man has opportunity to join during his life, I find this scenario hilarious.*

I could flirt with Taija and try to make her mine, but I'd be inflicting pain upon my close friend and roommate. Still, I could justify it by telling myself that I'd treat her better than he would...or that I need her more than he does. If I went that route, however, I'd be deluding myself, coating my spirit in filth, and falling into the bottom chamber.

Now I understand what makes staying on a righteous path so challenging—we can rationalize, justify, and find support for anything. William Shakespeare may have said it best in The Tragedy of Hamlet..."What a piece of work is a man! How noble in reason!" Living by morals can seem depressing and boring to those who don't see the Light. Have I seen the Light? My senses have awakened and my perception feels complete. I think the dusty shade that used to surround my inner lamp has been torn to shreds.

Jack heard Paco and Taija conversing about seeing a movie, and he began writing a short story entitled *Beyond Coincidence* while he waited for them to leave. After he heard the door close, he went into the dining area and ate the food that Paco had generously prepared for him. He ate it slowly, savoring each bite, for he was in no hurry to get anywhere. Then he went back to his room and noticed that his answering machine light was blinking. He listened to the message and was thankful to hear from his old friend.

"Hey Jack. It's Rod. I'm going to be in Tallahassee this weekend, and I thought you might be up for a little golf or a poker game. I'll call you to see what you're doin' when I get there."

It'll be good to see Rod again, Jack thought, *and maybe he'll bring a few lady friends with him. Well he's engaged, so his fiancée probably wouldn't be too excited about him spending time with other girls. Still, hanging out with Rod will be fun in and of itself. Tomorrow's Saturday...I won't get to see Potential-2 for a few days.*

Jack looked around his room for the powerful, all-natural sedative that never failed him. He found the textbook entitled *Financial Management of Today's Firm*. He read a few pages, got into bed, and fell asleep as soon as his head touched the pillow.

Habitual Creatures

"Human beings are creatures of habit. Foregoing our ingrained living patterns for the promise of better ones can be painful when undergone with the support of others and excruciating when undergone alone."
^ *from* the short story *Almost Set in Stone* by Jackson Muldoone

    Chloe awoke on Saturday to a cold bedroom. She looked next to her at Tony, deducing that he had woken up in the middle of the night and found need for the entire blanket. *He's sound, snug, snoring, and selfish. He's always selfish, even in his sleep. I love him anyway, though, because he needs someone like me to care for him, and I need to be needed.*
    She went onto her porch and smoked marijuana then came back inside her apartment. She wondered, *will I wake 'n' bake every morning for the rest of my life?* Feeling her senses awaken from the swift rush of dopamine, then feeling an inescapable hunger, she poured sugar-encrusted kid's cereal into a bowl and added milk from the fridge. Then she sat on her couch and turned on the TV, thinking of her boyfriend as she ate breakfast and watched cartoons.

Chloe Angela Nakhota was born in Dallas, Texas in 1980. Her father was an Americanized Sioux Indian. His name was Philip, and he was born and raised in South Dakota before moving to Dallas at the age of eighteen. There he met his wife on a blind date arranged by one of his colleagues at his environmental engineering firm. Chloe's mother was a beautiful nurse named Michelle, whose family had emigrated from France to the United States only a year before she met Philip.

Chloe's favorite childhood memory was when her father taught her how to ride a motorcycle. She was only eleven at the time, but she had ever since remembered that day vividly. Riding her father's Harley Davidson touring-style motorcycle around their neighborhood, she loved the freedom she felt. Her favorite thing to do was to change gear then accelerate with a firm hand twist. Her father loved her as much as a parent can love his or her child, and he always made sure that she wore a helmet, kept out of traffic, and never went over 30 miles per hour. But Chloe's father traded in the bike for a car only a few months after his daughter's first ride. She had ever since longed to find a boyfriend who owned a motorcycle.

Tony drove a motorcycle, and that was one of the things Chloe enjoyed about dating him. They had met at Tallahassee's RJ's Sports Bar when they both had worked there. When he was twenty-nine years old, Tony tended bar at the upscale establishment while Chloe waited tables. Chloe had quit her job and been unemployed for over a year; she was pursuing graduation from F.S.U. Tony quit his job at the bar a day after Chloe did, and then he took up the riskier, yet more profitable by his measure of the word, occupation of dealing drugs.

He dealt marijuana and ecstasy, while always keeping a good supply of both on hand for Chloe and himself. It was the drugs that kept their relationship together. Chloe knew this and occasionally longed for a purer love. She knew her life could be better, but she was comfortable around Tony, and she feared the loneliness that would follow separation from him. They had been together for eight months and were emotionally attached, but passion for one another could rarely be felt unless drug-induced.

After finishing her breakfast, Chloe drove to the art store in her black Toyota Celica convertible. She was an art major in college and had discovered before adolescence that her niche was painting and drawing. She painted in watercolor, oil, and acrylic, and she drew with both pencil and pastel. Because she was using acrylics as the medium in her current painting, she bought new tubes of the two paints she would use the most, mars black and titanium white.

Two weeks before, she had seen a flier on campus in the Art Department for a contest. This contest was being hosted by the Leon County Youth Fair officials, who were searching for a poster that could best portray the upcoming annual fair. They would then put pictures of the winning poster on their brochures and advertisements. Chloe had decided to enter the contest for both the $1,000 reward and the sheer thrill of having her work published. Her poster was more than half complete.

On the way back home, she saw Penelope's Pocket out her window. *That's where I played pool with that guy Jack freshman year*, she thought. *I wonder what happened to him. He was attractive and bright in conversation, but I just couldn't get any concept of the type of person he really was. Maybe he was just as nervous as me. I think he really liked me because he couldn't get that kid-in-a-candy-store smile off his face...He smiled throughout the whole evening. I remember being thrilled when he asked me out. There was something pleasantly different about him. I wonder what would've happened had we gone out again. Oh well, I'm with Tony now, and he satisfies my needs.*

Tony was still snoring when Chloe walked into their bedroom. *He looks like a fajita in that blanket*, she thought with a smile, *and I hope he's sizzling in it, too. I'm sure he'll be in bed all day...I told him not to eat three rolls last night because all that ecstasy would turn him into a zombie. Once he awakens he'll be a zombie, but right now he's a huffing-and-puffing, sizzling fajita.* Her smile became insidiously wicked. She considered pulling the tortilla-like blanket from him, but she figured it was best to let him sleep.

She brought her new paint tubes into her working room and set them near the easel with the other acrylics. *I'd better not confuse my oil-based paint for acrylics*, she thought. *Oil paint takes two years to dry sufficiently, and it never dries completely. My poster is due in one month for the contest, so I'd better get back to work.*

Chloe had already decided on her poster design and had painted about half of it. The focal point of her design was a central carousel being ridden by children. Surrounding it were other familiar carnival objects, such as a waffle cone of dripping cherry ice cream and a stand selling elephant ears and cotton candy. On the other side of the poster, there was an overflowing container of popcorn. In the distance was a roller coaster with the name "Certain Death" written in pencil at the top of its highest loop. Although it would make the poster less humorous, Chloe thought it would be best to change the name of the coaster to "Maelstrom" before painting it.

As Chloe delicately applied her brush to the poster board, she gradually saw all the components of her work coming together. While painting, the only sound she could hear was the discordant snoring of her boyfriend in the next room. Although she found that adorable for a short while, it began to annoy her, so she played a CD and closed the door of her workroom. She sang along with a quiet voice.

I didn't think about Tony even once during that song, she thought. *He must not be the one…but if I break up with him, who will be near me? I've paid enough loneliness dues in the past…I don't want to pay any more. Plus, I'd really miss his motorcycle.* She set her paintbrush onto a piece of aluminum foil, and then she went into the bedroom to see her boyfriend. He had rolled over to the center of the bed, and he was lying belly-down. His arm was outstretched over Chloe's vacated pillow, and he continued to sleep without even realizing that she had left his side.

Chloe sighed as she sat at her computer. She checked her e-mail and three new headings popped onto the screen. These headings were "Cheaper Long Distance Rates," "XXX Space Girls," and "Win a Trip to Antarctica." The only heading she took interest in was the one about winning a trip. *I love contests,* she thought, *but Antarctica seems like an unusual place for a weekend getaway. I'll have to see what this one's all about.* She double-clicked the heading and a new window opened on her screen—

"The F.S.U. English Department has teamed up with the F.S.U. Antarctic Marine Geology Research Facility to bring forth a contest. Ten bright F.S.U. students will have the opportunity of a lifetime—a weeklong trip to Antarctica! These students will fly to the Cape of Good Hope at the tip of South America then board the University's finest research vessel and cruise to Antarctica. These students will visit a research facility and sleep one night on the continent. This night will be during the winter solstice, and Antarctica will receive 24 hours of sunlight. Students will have the opportunity to see unique species of wildlife up close, and visit Mount Erebus, the world's southernmost active volcano!

The contest rules are as follows. Any current F.S.U. student who enters must submit a poem related either directly to Antarctica or to the trip in general. The poem can be of any style of verse, but its length must not exceed 100 lines. Judges from the English Department will select ten students based on the thought-provoking nature of their poems. We hope that all of you who would be thrilled to visit and learn about Antarctica enter this contest. Please send your poems to the F.S.U. English Department. The winners will be announced via e-mail three weeks from today."

That sounds incredible, she thought, *but I'm not a poet. I've gotta enter that contest, so I'll have to find a way to transfer my visual art skills to writing skills. Writing this poem will be like painting a landscape. My paper will be my canvas, my words will be my paint, my pen will be my brush, and my vocabulary will be my palette. I've gotta learn a lot about Antarctica before I can write this.*

She gathered some information from the Internet and an encyclopedia. She began by looking at an overall map of the continent, noticing first all the research stations. Then she found Mount Erebus along an ice shelf. *That's the volcano that was mentioned in the e-mail for the contest*, she remembered. *I can't believe I might actually have a chance to see it.* Looking again at the big picture, at the shape of the continent in its entirety, her mind transformed the white circle into an epic form.

Antarctica is shaped like a Native American spirit, she thought, *a winged angel with a feather protruding from the back of its head. The angel is spreading its wings around something, and looking down at it. It's looking at Mount Erebus! It's guarding it! Why does it watch over that volcano? Must be something important about it...it must contain some secret*. Then she read about the tilt of the earth, and she learned that there is no night during the winter solstice, as the sun is in the sky for 24 hours. *Midnight sun*, she thought. She went to the living area of her apartment, lay down on the couch, and—now with sufficient background information for her poem—she began to brainstorm.

She left the couch once the turning gears of her mind had produced some good ideas for a poem. Before beginning to write, she went inside her makeshift art studio and painted more of her poster. It was 5:30 in the afternoon, and she heard Tony get out of bed.

"Baby, where are you?" he asked.

"I'm in the studio, working on that poster I've been telling you about."

"Are you gonna cook breakfast?"

"Honey, the sun is about to go down, why don't we go out for dinner in a couple hours?"

"Dinner? But I just woke up. Can you be a sweetheart and cook me some scrambled eggs?

"Not right now," Chloe responded. "I'm busy, and I'm getting kinda tired of doing everything for you."

"Whatever babe. I'll just have some potato chips then," Tony said as he slowly opened the pantry door.

I wonder if there's a guy out there who'll treat me right, she thought, *someone who I need as much as he needs me. Well, I'll always have my artwork. That's what keeps me alive. I need to write this poem for the contest...what an adventure a trip to Antarctica would be.* She set her paintbrush down and found a pen. Then she opened the notebook that she had used in art history class and began forming verses on a blank page. After two more hours of contemplation and writing, she completed her poem:

How I long to bask in the midnight sun
In a land, though desolate, far from glum
A Great Spirit beckons me to this place
What I'd feel there, time could never erase
Down where glaciers in lieu of rivers run
Beneath a glorious and golden midnight sun

I wrote so few words, Chloe thought. *I hope the judges are looking for quality and not quantity...the former of which I hope my poem contains.* She put the poem into an envelope and mailed it to the F.S.U. English Department. She returned home from the post office and was about to ask Tony if he was ready for dinner, but then she heard him snoring in the bedroom. *I'll just have some cereal*, she thought as she sighed. After her not-so-satiating dinner, Chloe went inside her studio and stared at her poster. She looked at the children that she had painted. *They look so happy on that merry-go-round, so satisfied with life,* she thought. *I used to be like that, but that was before the drugs and long before this hollow relationship with Tony.* Chloe painted with emptiness in her chest, wishing the colors were as vibrant as they had been so long ago.

Destiny's Call

"Permitting the Light to illuminate my brain then pass through, I can subtly perceive the course of destiny."
^ *from* the short story *Finding the Smoothest Flow* by
Jackson Muldoone

Three weeks had passed since Chloe had begun her true longing for a more wholesome life. It had also been three weeks since Jackson had been visited by Rod. Jack and Rod had accomplished all they had planned on doing. They had moderately consumed the finest Tennessee and bourbon whiskies, played golf and cards, and had gone to a pool hall. Rod lightened Jack's wallet during the card games, but Jack reclaimed his lost cash in a friendly yet heated billiards match. After Rod had gone back home, Jack had become somewhat reclusive and had written a handful of short stories.

Jack had received the same e-mail that Chloe had, and as soon as he wrote an entry, he sent it to the English Department in hopes of winning the trip. As much as he disliked the win/lose nature of contests and competition, Jack thought they added an exciting dimension to life, and he saw the prospect of a voyage to Antarctica as the chance of a lifetime.

THE SANDS OF EREBUS

He had done a project on Mount Erebus in a geology class his freshman year, which sparked an intense yearning in him for this chance to witness the volcano's beauty first-hand. After an hour-long meditation and careful consideration, he had chosen to write a haiku incorporating all that he had learned about Mount Erebus. What intrigued him most about the volcano was the lava lake situated within its peak, amidst the ice. He had written and rejected a dozen haikus until he had been finally satisfied with the thirteenth passionate try. The waterfall had washed away his superstitions, so he no longer viewed thirteen as a foreboding number. He was pleased with his poem, and he thought it might have a chance:

Erebus
Ice encircles fire
All extremes there coexist
Essential message

The day of judgment had finally come, and his haiku kept soaring through his mind. *I'll get an e-mail today*, he thought, *either declaring me a winner or frustrating me to no end. Will my poem be good enough? Will the judges be able to read the passion between the lines? Ice encircles fire...so few words...so much desire.* While his heart beat like a jackhammer, pounding his ribs, he checked his e-mail every half-hour. In the early afternoon, an e-mail came, and it was *the* e-mail:

We are pleased to announce the winners of the Antarctica contest. They are as follows:

Mitsuru Atanusa	Jackson Muldoone
Andrea Chanel	Chloe Nakhota
Vishnu Fanji	Michelle Presnier
Jasmine McKey	Tristan Rindley
Sara Montcalm	Kaitlyn Sutherland

If your name is on this list, please speak with me in the English Department ASAP to confirm your place and get information concerning the upcoming trip. Thanks to each of you who entered this contest. All of the poems we read were deeply insightful, and it is unfortunate we could only select ten students. Best wishes on a great semester.

Sincerely,
Kenneth J. Cooper
Chairman, F.S.U. Department of English

Matthew R. Frost
Chief Operations Officer, F.S.U. Antarctic Marine Geology Research Facility

Jack's heart rate went beyond full-throttle into afterburner. "Chloe," he whispered with a long exhale. *Her name's right next to mine...is that a sign? I'm going on a weeklong trip with her! Has she seen my name? If not, she probably will soon. Will she even remember me? She will when we meet for the trip...but what'll I say to her? Any word from me will only taint her perfection. No! I can't think like that, or I'll never have a chance! What if she has a boyfriend? If so, I'd like to shake his hand then immediately proceed to punch him in the gut. No...I have to redirect negative emotions like these...jealousy and aggression would make quicksand below my feet...I'd sink into the chamber beneath...where those who act on impulse reside. I could certainly use a cigarette and a double gin-and-tonic right now.*

As he hastily smoked and drank on the patio, Jack started to come to grips with what was happening. Since the waterfall, he had been living peacefully as part of the Flow, but suddenly seeing Chloe's name made him realize that he could never live in the Smoothest Flow until he could cosmically blend with his true love. Lyrics to a song were emerging in his mind as he finished consuming his substances, so he came in from the patio and played the song at high volume. He sat in his desk chair and sang with passion.

Chloe, when I see you my heart will drop into my belly. Will I be able to even utter a word to you? He turned off his computer and went to the living area of his apartment. He watched a professional golf tournament on television in hopes of bringing calm back to his overexcited mind. Watching the gentle and noble game relaxed him a little, but he could neither keep a smile off his face nor his eyeballs in their sockets.

Once some more of his excitement wore down, Jack went to see if Dr. Cooper was in his office, even though it was Saturday. The English professor was there, and Jack confirmed his intent to go on the trip. After obtaining all the necessary information, he returned home and called his mother and father to share with them the news.

As he hung up the phone, it all began to sink in. *We leave only a month from now, during winter break,* he thought. *I won't be back until Christmas Eve…I'll miss Mom's cooking but everything has its cost. Maybe she'll cook the feast on Christmas Day instead of the eve. I can't imagine missing those deviled eggs and that turkey and stuffing.*

Chloe, he thought, *we are going to meet again…and soon.* He walked onto the patio and smoked a cigarette, thinking, *I'd rather be inhaling her sweet perfume…Destiny, I believe, was the name of her fragrance that evening so long ago.*

Antarctic Affluence

"Within the most inhospitable continent on Earth, human researchers and animals prosper. We must learn from their adaptability."
^ from the short story *Rewards of Determination* by Jackson Muldoone

It was December 17, 2001, the night before the voyage to Antarctica. Chloe had been arguing with her boyfriend ever since she told him about the trip. Tony was upset that she would be leaving him for a week. He did not trust her. That evening, he had sold drugs to three customers. One of them was an attractive girl who had traded sex for drugs. After cheating on Chloe for the tenth time, Tony came home and saw his girlfriend's luggage packed and ready by the front door.

"Hey!" he screamed at Chloe, who was back in her studio. "If you're going to pack for this trip, you'd better pack everything you own because I'll never want to see you again!"

"That's fine with me," Chloe responded, "I get only pain from you anyway!"

"Oh, you know I've treated you right. I'm the victim here," he proclaimed, seeking power through guilt. Then he went to the studio room to finish the confrontation face to face.

"That's bullshit!" Chloe screamed. "I'll sleep on the couch tonight, and I'll find another place to live as soon as I get back in town."

"You can sleep on the bed tonight if you want; I've already made other arrangements."

Chloe slammed the door right after Tony walked out of the studio. She sobbed as she put together what "other arrangements" must mean. *For a long time I thought he might be cheating on me with that slut,* she thought, *but I didn't want to believe it…she used to be my best friend!*

After crying on the floor of her studio for an hour, Chloe looked at her completed poster, which had won runner-up in the contest. She looked at the children riding the carousel. The smiles she had painted on the children's faces caused her to take a deep inhale. As she slowly exhaled, she made a promise to herself…*I'll never use drugs again.* Then she went to her room and put on boxer shorts and a loose-fitting tee-shirt. *I'll never again wear the lingerie he bought for me with his filthy money. I'll have to throw away everything he ever gave me, and then go shopping when I get back.* She lay in bed for a while, until a final thought gave her comfort as she fell asleep: *Jackson, I hope you still care for me.*

Jack awoke at 3:00am on the day of the voyage. Although he had rarely awakened before ten o'clock since he'd been in college, intense excitement had filled his mind while he was asleep. His excitement woke him hours before any rooster might call. He sat up in bed and looked at himself in his mirrored closet doors. *May I be an ace of hearts,* he prayed, *and may I see through to her inner self. May all go well, and may her spirit and mine unite.* He meditated until 8:00am then went to Waffle Mania for breakfast.

Chloe arrived at the Student Union—the meeting place—at 10:00am. She saw the other timely contest-winners and the researcher escorts/activity directors who would be guiding them. After introducing herself to everyone, she looked around for Jack. She saw someone walking toward the group from afar. *That's him,* she thought as her heart skipped a beat. *He's not as skinny as he used to be…he's put on some pounds in the past few years. What should I do when he gets here? It's going to be awkward no matter what...I'm gonna give him a big hug to let him know I care.*

There she is, Jack thought. *Ok, just pretend like my life hasn't revolved around the hope of this moment for the past month...err...three years. Try to read appropriately into her actions then blend accordingly.* As he neared her, he first noticed what he thought of as "hug-me" dimples in her cheeks. *Her smile is telling me to hug her, so I've got to.* He returned her smile with one of his, and then they hugged.

"How have you been?" she asked during the embrace.

"I've been good," Jack replied as he let her go. "How's your pool game? Last time we played I think you got the best of me."

"I haven't shot pool in a while, actually. I've been painting and drawing some. I never thought of you as the poet type, so I was surprised when I found out you won this thing."

"Yeah, me too. Actually I'm a business student, but I have more passion for writing than for accounting and whatnot. I write short stories and I'm about to start a novel. My dream is to get published, but I guess I've got to write some good ones first." *I'm rambling*, he thought. *Regain your composure, Jack.*

"We must have kindred spirits," Chloe said. "I think this trip is gonna be unbelievable."

"Yeah, me too. Antarctica must be an unusual place for vacations. This whole experience seems beyond any expectation."

"Almost surreal, isn't it? Visiting a frozen wasteland, reuniting with an old friend."

Oh no, Jack thought. *She dropped the friend bomb on me...old friend! That's the nuclear bomb. In reality, I guess that's all we'd established back then—a friendship. Maybe she lacked a better word. There is still hope...there must be. Fate has set the grand stage this one last time...I'd better not buckle.*

"I'd better make my rounds," Jack said. "It's great getting in touch with you again."

I'd love to touch her neck and kiss her forehead, he thought, *but it's not yet time for that. I'd also love to touch her hips and kiss her lips...if I can only play my cards right.*

Jack fought the fantasies while he got acquainted with everyone else in the group; everybody had now arrived. They packed the van and drove to the airport; Jack and Chloe sat together for the ride. They learned much about each other, and the more they learned, the more alike they came to realize they were. Jack told Chloe that he smoked cigarettes and she found common ground in their inhalation of burning plants.

Chloe told him about Tony, and that she had just broken up with him, and that she would have to find a new apartment. She told him that she had entered the art contest for the youth fair and how painting the poster had changed her. They spoke with each other about things in such a comfortable tone that a casual observer might think they had known each other their whole lives.

Jack told Chloe about his adventures at the waterfall in Georgia. He told her about his fascination with Mount Erebus ever since working on the geology project three years before. Chloe described to him what she saw in the map of Antarctica, how she gazed at it like a cloud-watcher and the shape of an angel took form.

After arriving at Tallahassee Municipal Airport, the group boarded a private jet. *I've seen this type of airplane in movies,* Jack thought. *It's a Gulfstream. Let the great current bring us to our destiny.* They flew for nine hours, making one stop to refuel in Lima, Peru before landing at Tierra Del Fuego, an island at the southern tip of South America. During the flight, Chloe sat next to Jack and napped most of the way. She had tossed and turned all throughout the previous night because of the crossroads of uncertainty at which she suddenly stood. Also, her breakfast that morning had lacked its usual THC fortification. While Chloe rested, Jack listened to music on his portable CD player. He was trying to distract his mind from obsessing over Chloe. Each song, however, only enriched his yearning for her touch.

Once the group deplaned, the activities directors led them to the bus that would take them to the research ship. They rode to the docks, and on the way Jack found some irony in the island's name. *This is Tierra del Fuego,* he thought, *Land of Fire. I'm freezing under this coat. If this is what the Land of Fire feels like, Antarctica will make this place seem like Miami Beach in July.*

Everyone in the group wore a heavy jacket, but they all knew that these jackets were like undershirts compared to what they would need on the frozen continent. They arrived at the ship, R/V Langston Hemingway, and Jack felt a sudden sense of déjà vu: *This red and black ship! It looks just like the one I saw on the horizon at South Beach. Ah, South Beach…it may as well be the North Pole from here.*

Everyone boarded the ship and was shown to his or her quarters. There was one cot in each cabin, and it was too small for Jack. He tested the bed and realized his feet were dangling off the end. *I'll have to make do,* he thought. *These researchers truly rough it out here. Well, I guess that when studying the farthest recesses of the planet, simple comfort becomes a luxury. I have an all-new respect for these scientists…they must have pure passion for their jobs, a yearning to discover. There are only "amenities" for one in this cabin, so I won't be sleeping with Chloe. Well, at least she has the room across the way. I'm so in love with her.*

Once everyone became acquainted with their new bedrooms, the ship departed. The Chief Operations Officer of F.S.U. Antarctic Research, Dr. Frost, took the students on a tour of the ship as they began their ocean journey. Jack and Chloe walked side by side while they learned about the ship. They spoke quietly with each other when Dr. Frost was not speaking. Now that Chloe was with him, Jack discovered the Smoothest Flow—he was living in the present without fear. She smiled at him and he noticed the softest brown eyes he had ever seen. Jack felt the mysteries of the universe begin to unfold…

During their two days at sea en route to Antarctica, Jack and Chloe gravitated toward each other both physically and spiritually. They arrived at Antarctica on December 21 and took a helicopter to McMurdo Station. After being assigned their sleeping quarters within the research facility, the group set out via snowmobile to see Mount Erebus. While driving on the ice, Jack's eyes hurt from the glare of the sun.

Light reflects off this ice just like it did off the Atlantic Ocean during my mornings on South Beach, Jack thought. *Even squinting, my eyes hurt, but I don't want to wear my sunglasses...it's such a pleasant pain.* The group dismounted their snowmobiles once arriving at the volcano, and they stood 500 yards from its base.

"We can't go up to the crater rim to see the lava lake," said Dr. Frost, "because there is too much seismic activity taking place at this time. If we're lucky, we'll see a lava bomb fly out of the crater. If we're really lucky, it won't land on us and pound us into a frozen grave. Ha, just kidding a bit with you all. We're safe here."

Erebus, Jack pondered. *That was the name given to the son of Chaos in Greek mythology. Erebus was believed to be the embodiment of the Underworld. My middle name...Brandon...means "of the fiery hill". This volcano is part of me.*

It's like an Indian burial mound, Chloe thought. *That's why the Great Spirit protects it. I want my body to be placed in the lava lake when I die. One of my grandfathers was buried...the other was cremated, and my aunt was lowered into the Pacific Ocean, a bubbling mass of liquid. I'd like to sample all three...but this is not the time for thoughts of death. Jack will bring me new life, a fresh hope.*

Just as Chloe finished her contemplation, a large pool of molten rock ejected from the crater. The liquid froze in the extremely sub-zero air and landed on the side of the mountain with a "thud." *This mountain is open,* Jack thought, *it has an unsealed summit...no completion...no complacency.* He looked to the sky then asked Dr. Frost a question: "Are there ever clouds in the sky here?"

"Antarctica is the largest desert in the world. Snow rarely falls over our land."

He called it our land, Jack thought. *He has been studying this world with so much passion that he has become an integral part of it.*

"Let's take our icemobiles over to the coast," Dr. Frost said in a guiding voice, "and let's see if we can find some penguins."

The group drove to the edge of the Ross Ice Shelf. A large flock of penguins was living there. Some were swimming, some were playing, and some were basking. *There must be ten thousand of them,* Jack thought. *Looks like young, old, and teenagers alike among them. A society so rich, thriving in the badlands of Earth...there is so much from them to be learned.* Some of the penguins left the flock and began belly sliding toward Mount Erebus, and others walked back from it to rejoin their colleagues.

Led by Dr. Frost, the students headed back toward McMurdo Station. *These icemobiles are more fun than motorcycles*, Chloe thought. *Maybe some day I'll live in the tundra and ride one from place to place. Maybe Jack could ride with me...with me forever.* They got back to the research base and relaxed there to thaw out and soak in all that they had seen. Chloe looked outside and noticed that the sun had descended in the sky, almost to the horizon.

"Jack, do you wanna watch the midnight sun with me?" Chloe asked.

"Definitely. Is it time yet?"

"Yup, come on."

Chloe reached out her hand and Jack connected with her.

"I'm surprised your warmth doesn't melt this place", he said. "You could make Florida go underwater."

Jack's flattering comment produced a smile on Chloe's face. They went outside the station alone and sat on the ice. They watched the sun approach the horizon from an angle then softly bounce back into the sky, as if dawn and dusk had become one. As the sun rose, Chloe pulled back her hood and looked at Jack with a hunger in her eyes. *It's time to kiss her*, he thought. *It's now or never.* He pulled back his hood. Their lips were trembling and frozen blue as they leaned in. They kissed inseparably for a full hour.

The heat from their kiss thawed their lips to a scarlet crimson. They both felt a peculiar spark in their brains, as if a great switch, which had been off all their lives, suddenly had been flipped on. While they sat in a one-armed-embrace, reflecting upon the thorough enjoyment of their kiss, Jack knew it was time to make a proposal to Chloe.

"I want you to live with me when we get back to school" Jack offered. "You're the best thing that's happened to me in a long time."

"I would *love* to be with you, Jack. For years, my feelings for you have been concealed in the depths of my soul. They've come out of hiding."

Chloe and Jack went inside the station and hugged. It was an embrace of pure completeness.

"Sleep well, adorable one," said Jack.

"You too, ecstasy."

They parted and lay in their beds to reflect. After Chloe went to sleep, Jack put his freezer suit back on and went outside for a cigarette. *I've lost all sense of self*, he thought. *It's as though I have become us.* He finished his cigarette and touched its burning tip to the ice. Then he went inside and threw away the filter before going to bed. He and Chloe slept more peacefully that night than ever before.

Dr. Frost awakened the group nine hours later. They took the helicopter to the ship and headed to the Island of Fire. Aboard the ship, Jack wrote a letter to his mother, which he planned on sending her by e-mail once he got back to Tallahassee. That way, she could read it while he drove home to Miami on Christmas Day.

> Dearest Mom,
> Oh, I have seen the blending of contrasts here. Here in Earth's most inhospitable badlands, I have seen nothing but good. I have seen red-hot blobs of molten lava explode out of a volcano. I have seen these blobs solidify in the biting-cold air before hammering the thickest of ice. I have seen the sun try to set but fail, then realized the miracle of its failure. I have worn ten thousand layers of wool without breaking a sweat. I have spoken with people whom I could hardly see through opaque breath.
> I have united with the woman of my dreams. I hope she will continuously pour nutrients into my soul. Dad and you have always been my safety net, without which I could not have walked the tightrope of love. And ah yes, I have seen the penguins, Mom. They are both black and white. They are as sharply contrasted as Erebus's lava lake, which boils unfazed by the surrounding cold. Oh, I have seen the

penguins, how they subtly coexist in a climate most extreme. I have seen them, and I have seen how we can all be free.

   Love,
   Jackson

Just before he wrote the letter, Jack had lent Chloe his CD player with his favorite album inside, *Enigma 3*. She selected song seven, for that was her lucky number. In bed she lay, listening to the smooth music while watching Jack's half-opened door across the way—

"Some day you came
And I knew you were the one
You were the rain, you were the sun
But I needed both, 'cause I needed you

You were the one
I was dreaming of all my life
When it's dark, you are my light
But don't forget who's always our guide

It is the child in us"

Printed in the United States
50927LVS00006B/574-594